How to Whistle
Expanded Edition

Gregg Shapiro

PRAISE FOR
HOW TO WHISTLE

"Gregg Shapiro's *How to Whistle* brings to vibrant life young gay men's casual/intimate/kinky explorations of Boston, D.C., and Chicago in the 1980's. Deadpan humor alternates with delicious dish and quiet introspection in this witty collection of stories about sex, relationship, (in)fidelity, vengeance, and the meaning of friendship in a sometimes dangerous world. An entertaining, deeply insightful, and warmly nostalgic portrait of the way we were."

 – **Daniel M. Jaffe**, author of *Foreign Affairs: Male Tales of Lust & Love*

"Shapiro's *How to Whistle* documents the 1980s with sharp observation, humor, and keen insights. A decadent decade when urban tastes and desires "lit in a faint orange glow" knew no boundaries, friends and lovers being rushed to the hospital was a typical lunchtime conversation, and pop icons went from tragic to martyred saints of the bullied. This short story collection is also an homage to 1980s Boston and Chicago, as hip as Tama Janowitz' Manhattan in *Slaves of New York*, and as raw and sexy as Bret Easton Ellis' L.A. in *Less Than Zero*."

 – **R. Zamora Linmark**, author of *The Importance of Being Wilde at Heart*

"Shapiro's stories capture the breadth and variety of human relationships – friends, lovers and family; casual and deep; social and sexual. Funny, sad, tragic, and full of surprises, they will keep you reading to the very end and wanting more."

 – **John D'Emilio**, author of *Queer Legacies: Stories from Chicago's LGBTQ Archives*

"Gregg Shapiro writes with sincerity and verve about the greatness of our human joys and quandaries – love, sex, fear, friendship families of origin and families of choice. His love of narrative is always apparent in these stories, and his love of poetry lingers in every small facet of experience he takes the time to enlarge and lovingly render. For instance: "He crouched and touched the word Zenith, the Z like a lightning bolt underlining the rest of the letters." For instance, "I don't just hail any cab, I wait for one of those new ones that look like whales on wheels." And" "He is still wearing his white socks which seem to glow fluorescent against his black sheets." The power and beauty of *How to Whistle* resides in the details."

 – **Julie Marie Wade**, author of Just an Ordinary *Woman Breathing* and *Same-Sexy Marriage: A Novella in Poems*

Rattling Good Yarns Press
33490 Date Palm Drive 3065
Cathedral City CA 92235
USA
www.rattlinggoodyarns.com

Cover Design: Rattling Good Yarns Press

ISBN: 978-1-7341464-7-9
Library of Congress Control Number: 2021930280

Second Edition

Dedicated to my mother, Shirel Shapiro, and to the memory of my aunt, Darlene Shapiro Kaufmann (1939-2019).

CONTENTS

AUTOGRAPHS

The night Maggie and I went to see Adam and The Ants at The Paradise, there were hardcore kids with shaved heads, ripped jeans and flannel shirts tied around their waists, carrying signs that read: Black Flag Kills Ants On Contact. Their laced-up army boots sounded like fists making contact with the sidewalk as they picketed like experienced union members on strike.

Maggie lit a joint and passed it to me. We were already pretty stoned, having smoked a pipeful at my apartment before we left for the concert. Joe, my lover, wasn't interested in going to the show, drinking the two-drink minimum or spending any more time with Maggie than he had to.

"I almost met Henry Rollins," Maggie said in that voice she always got after taking a hit of a joint.

"Almost," I said, breathing the smoke in through my nose before toking on it.

"Really," Maggie said, her eyes bloodshot and wide. "They were playing at The Rat and..."

"Tony was going to get you backstage passes, but you had to work," I cut her off, finishing her sentence and exhaling at the same time.

"Almost fine," Maggie said, "just don't forget who got you backstage for the Go-Go's."

"Backstage. End of story. Just don't forget who backed you up when you told everyone you slept with Belinda Carlisle. Nodding off together doesn't count."

"That one's kind of cute," Maggie said, pointing at the punk parade, her short attention span already exhausted.

1

"Which one?" I asked, having a hard time telling the skinheads apart.

"That one," she said, pointing randomly at the crowd. "You having an L&M moment or can I have the joint back?"

Suddenly, Maggie started rummaging in her purse. It was an old leather shoulder bag, big enough for a change of clothes. She pulled out her transistor radio and held it to her ear without turning it on.

"I just know `BCN is playing 'Planet Earth' right now, I can feel it in the air."

"'Chihuahua,'" I said, wondering if or when she was going to turn it on.

"No, wait, it's 'The Magnificent Seven,'" she said, holding the radio so close to her ear, I was sure it would leave an impression, scar her for life, give her something to tell her grandchildren about.

"'What Does Sex Mean To Me?,'" I said, so confident in my choice that I would have kissed one of the skinheads on the mouth in a bet.

"Oh, for crissakes," someone behind us said. "just turn the radio on."

We were both wrong, as Ric Ocasek sang "Candy-O/I need you so," and the rest of The Cars harmonized. She turned it off and put it in her purse almost as quickly as she had taken it out.

"Gotta save the batteries," she said to me and anyone else within earshot.

"How did you get tonight off, anyway?" I asked. Maggie was known for the excuses she made up, and our boss, Dom, was known for believing them.

"Jackie wanted my hours. She needs to buy Oliver new shoes."

Maggie, Jackie and I waited tables in a dive near North Station called Café Society. We called it, Café Sociopath, because of our boss, Dom, and his twenty-year-old son and business partner, Rod. Also, because most of the customers were either patients or therapists at the Nut House, across the street.

Jackie was my age and had a two-year-old son, named Oliver. Maggie was a year younger and lived with her mother Marianne, who we called "the virgin Marianne," in an apartment cluttered with religious tracts and icons across from the State House. Jackie and Oliver lived in Charlestown, in the projects. I lived in the North End, with my lover, Joe. We lived above a twenty-four-hour bakery. Joe worked as a paralegal at a big law firm and when I wasn't waiting tables at Café Society, I was a college student.

"Oliver seems to be growing faster than Jackie can keep him clothed," I said, waving at a girl from my Western Civ class.

"Who's that?" Maggie asked, sounding like she almost cared.

"Someone from school. I don't remember her name."

"You've got this thing about names, don't you?" Maggie half-asked.

"I remember yours, don't I? Don't complain."

"I'll bet you don't remember the name of that new guy, the one Jackie's working with tonight."

"Scott," I said, guessing. "No, Stewart, Stan, Sven." I was shooting in the dark.

"Wrong," Maggie said, an unmistakable grin of victory on her face, and then she began to sing the Rockpile song, "Let's face it, you're wrong again."

"Well, whatever his name is, I hope Jackie isn't being too hard on him. I remember my first night with her."

Yeah, I remember my first night with her like it was last night. Dom was showing me around the kitchen, explaining all my responsibilities and duties to me. He was going on about how he liked having college kids working for him more than he liked locals. College kids are less likely to steal from me, he said. I asked him how many college kids he'd had working for him and he told me I was the first.

Jackie came stumbling into the kitchen. When she saw Dom, she straightened up as if she was a marionette and someone pulled a string in her back and shoulders. Dom introduced us and left. I'd never met anyone like her. She was beautiful and shrewd. She'd grown up in the West End and had been in trouble since she could remember. She had this thing for guys with criminal records. Most of her boyfriends were in prison, going to prison, or just getting out. Most of her boyfriends, that is, except for the father of her son, Oliver.

He was from a well-connected North End family. He worked in a bakery on Prince Street and dealt drugs on the side. When Jackie got pregnant, he offered to marry her, but he just wasn't enough trouble for her. Go hold up a convenience store and then maybe we'll talk, she told me she told him. I learned all this about Jackie within the first five minutes of talking to her. Her parents had moved into a new condo on Atlantic Avenue, a few blocks from where Joe and I lived, after the demolition of the West End had begun. She'd stop by our place unannounced, after visiting her mother and stepfather, but we both liked her and didn't mind the interruption. She told us she had a thing for gay men, they knew the real meaning of trouble.

Sometimes she'd bring Oliver with her after a visit. He was remarkably blonde for having parents with such dark hair and features. Joe had just discovered photography as a hobby, and Jackie and Oliver were more than happy to sit for him while he snapped and flashed away at them.

Maggie and Jackie weren't allowed to work together anymore on account of the "muffin melodrama," a run-in with Dom's perpetually stoned son Randy, who we called the "muffin man." Randy worked the night shift, cranking out muffins for the morning rush-hour crowd. He was older than Rod, who was Dom's business partner. Randy didn't seem to mind his station in life. He was the first person my age I'd ever met who hadn't finished high school.

When it was slow, Maggie and Jackie smoked weed with Randy in Dom's office. All the restaurant smells masked the marijuana smoke fairly well. One night, Jackie came in with a joint of angel dust and wouldn't let Randy smoke with her and Maggie. You would have thought the world was coming to an end. He began throwing baking utensils around the kitchen. Big silver bowls, muffin tins and mixing devices clanged against the walls and other surfaces. While Maggie was dialing 911 on the phone near the cash register at the front counter, Randy was calling Dom at home in Marblehead.

Surprisingly enough, the police got there first. In typical Dom fashion, money exchanged hands, and everything was forgotten. Everything except the work schedule. And even though Maggie and Jackie were prohibited from working together, that didn't stop either one of them from stopping in on their nights off, when the other one was working, and the tormenting of Randy continued.

Joe, my lover, thought Rod was to die for. Rod thought Joe was a little old and aggressive. Rod and I had a special "working relationship." Rod had just gotten married to Beth, a girl he had gotten pregnant while they were still in high school. He was about 6'2, with blonde hair and a slightly chipped front tooth. He had been a gymnast in high school, and he had muscular arms with big veins. He liked to wear tight-fitting, colored pocket tees. He told me I was the first homo he had ever met and if he'd met me sooner, things might have turned out differently.

I reminded him that he was a married man and soon-to-be a father, again. What I didn't tell him was that I dreamed about him all the time. We flirted in that weird way that gay men flirt with straight men. Everything was a double entendre. We touched a lot, and even though I'd been completely faithful to Joe, I was excited about being close to Rod, brushing past him in the kitchen or behind the pastry counter.

One time, after closing, while I was refilling the fluorescent-lit case with freshly baked tarts, Rod came up behind me. I was kneeling, reaching into the brightly lit shelves, when I sensed his presence. I started to stand up, slowly, and he put his long-fingered hands on my hips, as if to help me up. After I had stood all the way up, he kept his hands where they were and pulled me into him. We stayed that way for almost a minute, the seat of my jeans pressed up against his hard crotch. I could hear Randy singing along off-key with the radio in the kitchen.

"Randy," I said.

"No, Rod," Rod said and laughed.

"I know who you are," I said, "what if Randy sees us?"

"He'll be jealous," Rod said, and then he let go.

A few weeks later, after our flirting seemed to have died down a bit, I was in the stockroom taking inventory, when Rod walked in and closed the door behind him. Dom was still in his office, counting the lunchtime receipts. Maggie was fighting with Floyd, one of the cooks.

"Your boyfriend called," Rod said, leaning against the door. "I told him you were busy. Are you busy?"

"Kind of," I said.

I was sitting on a stack, three-high, of twenty-pound muffin-mix bags. Bran, corn, blueberry. I was just about eye-level with Rod's basket, which appeared to be in full bloom under his Jordache jeans. Something in his eyes, blue-grey and shiftier than usual, told me this visit was more than an employer checking up on an employee and less than a social call.

"I haven't had sex in so long, Maggie is beginning to look good to me," he said, hands on slim hips, his Chuck Taylored foot tapping.

At first, I thought about defending Maggie, brushing off Rod's advances, but my tongue took over.

"Look at what happened the last time you had sex."

"Wait a minute," he said, on the defensive, sense of humor vaporized, "we've had sex since then. It's just that one of Beth's girlfriends told her that it wasn't good for the fetus if we fucked. Besides, she's a good Catholic girl, so the back door is out of the question."

"Why don't you ask her doctor? I'm sure he'll tell you it's okay."

"I don't WANT to have sex with Beth," he said, his voice trailing off in an invitation.

"Here?" I said, not letting any time pass, "Right now? With your father on the other side of that wall? With Maggie and Floyd starting World War III out there?" I was gesturing wildly, pointing in all directions at once. The legal pad rocked in my lap.

He stepped away from the door, closer to me. I stood up, too quickly, and swooned from the moment and lack of oxygen in the stock room. He reached out to me, to help me regain my balance, and pulled me against his chest. I crashed into his pecs and immediately wanted to stay there forever.

Forever lasted about twenty seconds. There was a knock on the door.

"Roddie, honey, are you in there?" It was Beth.

"Yeah, Babe, be right out. Just helping Gabe with the inventory."

Maggie, Jackie and I called Beth, the Blue Ox, because Rod called her Babe. I wanted him to call me Babe, but I knew we'd never have the chance for this again. Beth distrusted me, and soon Rod would become preoccupied with fatherhood, again. When he opened the door and walked out into the kitchen, Prince was singing "Dirty Mind" on the radio.

I'd never told Maggie or Jackie about the "stockroom incident." I wanted to tell Joe, but things were a little rocky in our relationship, and I was afraid that telling him would only result in the impending avalanche. I looked at Maggie, who was shifting her weight from leg to leg, growing increasingly bored with waiting on line. Now was not the time.

One of the doormen from the Paradise appeared at the head of the line. He was thick with muscle and fat. He held a bullhorn in one hand and a piece of paper in the other. He held the piece of paper close to his face and began to read from it in his Southie accent. We could hear him just fine from where we stood, but somebody near the end of the line yelled, "Use the bullhorn, asshole."

"Oh, sorry," he said, remarkably polite for someone of his size and bulk.

"May I have your attention, please," he continued in that vein, "due to the overwhelming popularity of tonight's act and the careless overselling of tickets, the concert has been relocated to Metro on Lansdowne Street. The show will begin in one hour. Your tickets will be honored at the door. We regret the inconvenience."

Then, just as quickly as he'd appeared, he ducked into the club. This was a wise move on his part; between the picketing skinheads and the restless patrons, he could have been reduced to a pulp.

"Oh, great," Maggie said, "we got here early so that we could get a good seat, now every latecomer asshole on line is going to get there before we do."

"Not if we walk fast," I said and grabbed her hand, pulling her out of line and across Commonwealth Avenue.

We managed to set a pretty good pace, passing people on all sides. A couple of times we had to slow down as Maggie lit joints and cigarettes. Of course, we had to stop at the Store 24 for something to drink and munch on. As we passed the Nickelodeon Cinema, I knew we were home free.

Once inside Metro, our tickets collected and Adam and The Ants tour t-shirts purchased, we found a spot at the foot of the stage to stand. We ordered drinks from Zelda, our favorite barmaid, and danced to whatever the DJ played. Maggie had a habit of burning holes in other peoples' clothes with her cigarettes while she danced, so I gave her plenty of room.

The last time we were here, to see our favorite local band, The Fences, we almost got thrown out, because Maggie insisted on smoking a joint the size of a Cuban cigar. I wanted to remind her about this, but it was still a touchy subject. I also figured that she was sufficiently stoned and wouldn't need any more until after the show.

I was wrong, of course. In the middle of "Antmusic," Adam and The Ants' fourth song of the set, Maggie was digging around inside her Marlboro box for the joint of dust Jackie had given her.

"Where the fuck is it?" Maggie shouted at me.

"Maybe your mother has it," I said. "Maybe she was expecting a visit from God tonight and needed a little something to get her in the mood."

"Here it is," she said, ignoring my last remark.

"Please don't, Maggie. I don't want to get thrown out."

"Don't be such a limp dick," she said. "If you don't want any, just say so."

"I don't want YOU to have any," I said. "I don't want to have another bouncer confrontation. If you must smoke it, go into the bathroom."

"And miss the concert? Are you kidding?"

Sure enough, just as she was taking that first long drag, a big, burly bouncer named Bruno came up behind her and tapped her ever so daintily on the shoulder. She squinted her eyes into slits and offered it to him. He took it, dropped it onto the floor and crushed it.

"What the fuck did you do that for, you big ape?"

He started to walk away. Maggie went after him. I grabbed her by the purse strap. She swung around, her drink making an arc of Canadian Club and ginger ale over the crowd. We were nose to nose, in the middle of an angry and damp circle.

"Maggie, pick up the fucking joint, put it in your purse and behave yourself."

Her eyes were wide and wild. We glowered at each other. I kissed her on the cheek to break the ice. She folded her arms across her chest, turned to face the stage and stayed that way for the rest of the concert. She was the only body not swinging or swaying to the music. By the end of the show, she was leaning against me, softly snoring on her feet.

It was late and we'd have to walk fast to catch the last train out of Kenmore Square station. Once outside, the fresh air seemed to revive Maggie. She was awake, walking briskly, but silent. I tried to make conversation, talk about the concert, Adam Ant's hip-hugging leather pants, Marco's drumming. Anything, but an apology. I didn't think I should be sorry for preventing her from getting thrown out, face down in front of 10 Lansdowne Street.

"We should have gone to the after-concert party at Spit." It was the first thing she'd said to me since I rescued her.

"You should have said something sooner."

"I was still mad at you. I can't talk to you when I'm mad."

We were on our way downstairs, into the subway station. I had a token in one hand and the ticket stub from the concert in the other.

"Let's go back," I said, "we just have to show them the stub at the door."

"How will we get home? I spent my cab fare on the t-shirt and drink."

"Me, too," I said. So, I guess our decision was already made for us.

The train that pulled into the station was making its last stop at Park Street. We had just missed the Government Center Station train that would have left us in between our houses. We'd spent many a night saying goodbye on the brick plaza in front of City Hall; Maggie walking away towards Beacon

Hill, me heading off toward the glowing spire of the Old North Church in the North End.

The train wasn't too crowded, there were seats available when we first got on, but Maggie insisted on walking through both cars to see if we knew anybody. As luck would have it, we did, sort of.

Sitting in the back of the second car, all by himself, was Bob Wire, lead singer of our favorite local band The Fences. Maggie and I were walking next to each other down the aisle. The seats in front of Bob Wire were empty. We moved towards them as if they had a weird gravitational pull.

"Oh, my God, oh, my God, oh, my God," Maggie was babbling, a second wind in effect.

"Sssh," I said, trying to be the more mature and responsible one, while my leg was bobbing up and down in uncontrollable excitement.

"Oh, my God, it's Bob Wire. Bob Wire takes the T. Oh, my God, I can't believe it. How do I look?"

I looked at Maggie. Even stoned and tired, she was stunning. Her long, blonde hair parted in the middle still looked freshly washed, even though it smelled of cigarette smoke and a nightclub. Her eyes were tamer than they were earlier. Blue and less bloodshot. Her cheeks were flushed, rosy and just-pinched looking. She was wearing tight-fitting Levi's and a New England Aquarium t-shirt, old and faded and stretched over her breasts. If I was a lesbian, I could have gone for her in a big way.

"You look fine," I said.

Maggie and I took turns taking what we thought were inconspicuous peeks and glances at him over our shoulders. He was reading a dog-eared copy of *Rolling Stone*. He didn't seem to be aware of our fawning.

"Ask him for his autograph," Maggie whispered.

"Why don't you?" I asked.

"I'm too nervous. Besides, you're the guy."

"What does that have to do with anything? You're butch, why don't you ask him?"

"Oh, my God, what if he gets off at Auditorium or Copley Square?"

"Why don't you ask him where he's getting off?" I suggested.

"Come on, ask him for an autograph. Pleeeeeeease."

What could I possibly ask him to autograph? All I had was my ticket stub and the WBCN bumper sticker they gave us at Metro.

"Do you have any paper in your purse? A page from your journal or something?"

"No, I cleaned out my purse before I left tonight. I didn't know we were going to have a brush with greatness."

After she said that, Maggie turned around and offered Bob Wire her most seductive smile. He was oblivious. The train stopped at Auditorium, Copley Square, Arlington Street, Boylston Street. Bob Wire stayed in his seat, turning pages. The next stop would be Park Street, the last.

"Park Street Station," the conductor said, his voice remarkably audible for the hour. "Last stop, everybody off."

We got up from our seats and stepped into the aisle. Bob Wire was still sitting down. Maggie poked me in the ribs. I shrugged my shoulders.

"Last stop," the conductor said, again, "everybody off."

Bob Wire stood up and stretched as if his alarm clock had just woken him and he was getting out of bed and heading for the shower. He walked a little unsteadily up behind Maggie and me. Maggie poked me in the ribs, again.

"Say something," she hissed.

We were standing at the top of the stairs on the train. Maggie got off first, and while I still had both feet on the last step, I turned around and thrust the bumper sticker and a pen into Bob Wire's chest.

"Uh...can I...can we have your autographs...I mean autograph?"

I caught him completely off guard.

"Well, yeah, sure...I...uh...I'm kind of stoned right now..."

"Oh, my God," Maggie yelped like a dog whose tail had just been stepped on, "so are we."

He was still standing on the steps of the train when the conductor tried to close the door. Maggie reached her hand in and pulled him off, beaming as if she had just saved him from certain death. He landed, cat-like, on his feet, and looked at Maggie kind of funny.

"Uh, thanks...who are you?"

"Oh, my God," Maggie started in, "we're like your biggest fans. I mean, we think The Fences are wicked good. Like, we're always calling `BCN to request 'The First Lady Song' and 'Who Killed Marilyn?'

"Is that right? Well, thanks. What I meant was who should I make the autograph out to? What's your name?"

"Oh, well, I'm Gabe and this is Maggie. Mr. Wire, sir."

"Just call me Bob," he said, "my mother does."

"Just call him Bob," Maggie echoed, as if they were old friends.

He handed me the bumper sticker, which he signed on the back. I was sure Maggie was going to offer him a breast to sign, but she surprised me when she handed him her ticket stub.

"Adam and The Ants?" he said, examining the front of the stub.

"Oh, it was a really lousy show," Maggie said, defensively, and then she was off, "they were free tickets, from my ex-boyfriend Tony. I'm a lesbian now, I mean I don't hate men or anything, but when I was with Tony he was always getting me tickets for shows. He works at that used record store on Newbury Street. Maybe you know him. Anyway, I almost met Henry Rollins, once, but I had to work. We did get to go backstage when the Go-Go's played. You see I have this wicked crush on Belinda Carlisle and…"

BATHERS

1. GETTING THERE

He needs an escort, someone with experience in the darker regions, for various reasons. A partner-in-crime, who backs out at the last minute, but issues a warning before pushing him out of a moving car.

"Don't look so wide-eyed," was all he said.

He practices squinting as he walks. On the way, he passes a slab of wet cement. He wants to leave his handprints, his name, the date. This night must be one he'd always remember. He forgets, through the flickering neon, up the worn, carpeted stairs. He fumbles in his pocket, pressing the folded tens. The money is still there, next to the coins, which he nicknames Courage, and jangles like worry beads. Sweat builds up on his upper lip, his forehead. He mumbles through the registration, staggers through the security door.

2. ROOM 27

Four flights up. Past the laundry room, rows of lockers, the showers, the toilets, the VD clinic. Up to the television room, the sauna, the playroom. Up, again, to narrow cubicle-lined halls, doors with enormous numbers painted on them. Shag carpeted corners, elevated and wide enough for two.

The guide points out fire exits, his body temperature rises. He keeps startling himself with his own reflection in too many mirrors to count. Still higher, to the top floor with more cubicles and a spiral staircase leading to the roof, which is locked in October.

Inside room 27 is a cot, covered with a plastic sheet, a pillow and linens. He dims the harsh orange light which hangs over a small, square mirror mounted at the foot of the cot. When his eyes became accustomed, he drops his towel on the cot. Undressed, he wraps the towel around his waist, puts the elastic key ring around his wrist and lights a cigarette. In the dim orange glow of the light, his face seems less pale, more confident.

3. BATHERS

There is no shortage of men, this October Indian Summer night. Their urban tastes and desires know no boundaries. Men of all ages roam each floor. No two men wear their towels at the same length. One man wears a black, lace teddy, fish net stockings, garters and treacherously high heels. He lounges in a corner, chain-smoking pink cigarettes.

Every second or third door opens to reveal a solitary man or a couple, inviting those who happen by to join in or watch. He needs to comb each floor, commit each face to memory. He is a mouse in a maze, searching for the perfect piece of cheese. A radio station plays oldies and requests, fills the air with rhythms and voices.

In the television room, the colored TV plays to the walls. The sauna is dark and forbidding, the windows thick with steam. A shower is running, and the playroom is vacant, eerie with a pale blue glow. At the staircase leading to the third floor, he encounters two older men, both balding, whose eyes follow him, while their heads never turn.

Up to the fourth floor, around the spiral staircase. He glances at the closed door, room 27. Four doors away from the doorless main activity room at the end of the hall. Inside, it's dark, dimly lit by two blue lights at either entrance. It takes his eyes a minute to adjust, focus, survey. He's not alone in the semi-darkness. The shapes look like shadows. He hesitates, turns at the sound of suckling. His knees buckle and he walks before he falls.

It is better lit in the hall. The men he passes seem to be in a trance. In the television room, he's only conscious of a series of commercials, talking heads, lousy reception. The glow from the television lights him like a candle. On the first floor he passes the laundry room, glowing fluorescent white, deceptively sterile. The machines hum like nerves. It is deserted, except for the man at the front desk, smoking a cigarette, reading the newspaper. He manages to avoid or ignore the eyes of the men he encounters on his way back to the fourth floor.

This time, he enters the main activity room from the other side. There is only one man, standing in the center of the room, between two huge mattresses. He squeezes one of his nipples, fondles himself through his towel. He stands in front of him. The man stops what he is doing, puts both of his hands on his chest, slowly slides them down. The man opens his towel, drops to his knees. He stares straight ahead in the dark. Pretends that the man in front of him is young, his age or younger. He puts his hands atop the other man's head, feels his thinning hair, barely covering his scalp. He pulls away.

4. THE COST OF LOVE

Back in the television room, an old man with glasses watches *Magnum, P.I.* – Tom Selleck walks down a strip of Hawaiian beach. The old man inches closer to him. He pretends not to notice; his eyes glued to the glowing tube. When the old man gets close enough, he glances at him out of the corner of his eye. His hair is white, the hair on his chest, too. He stares at him. His eyes move down his chest to the towel, his legs, his feet, back up again to his face. He sits stone still. Only his eyes move. Back and forth, from the old man to the television set. He moves his legs a little and the towel parts at the thigh, exposing a hint of what is underneath. Suddenly, he gets up, startling the old man, whose eyes return to the TV.

The few doors on the third floor that are open cast a faint orange glow into the hall. Two younger men stand in one of the doorways to the main activity room on the fourth floor. He turns around and heads for the other entrance. A man moans from behind a closed door. Before his eyes can adapt to the change in lighting in the main activity room, he feels a familiar hand on his arm. It is the same man from earlier.

The man's hand drops to his, sticks a bill into it. "Twenty dollars," he whispers, still holding his hand. He leads him to one of the mattresses. He can still make out the silhouettes of the two men in the doorway. He closes his fist tightly around the twenty. The man opens his towel and he slides back on the mattress. The man's towel opens as he lies down next to him. He comes sooner than he wants to, lets go of him, sits up. He finds his hand in the semi-darkness and puts the twenty back.

5. HOME BY 10

Sitting naked on the cot in room 27, elbows on his knees, head in his hands. The room spins, stops, then spins again. Someone is talking about him. His ears burn, ring. In the next room, someone groans, grunts.

He dresses slowly, as if he's just learned how to do it. He has trouble tying his shoes. Puts his jacket on, slings his knapsack over his shoulder. He hands in his towel at the registration desk and the guy in the laundry room asks him where the sheets are. He tells him he didn't use them.

"It doesn't matter," the laundry room attendant says, "they still have to be washed." He apologizes, embarrassed, and goes back up to room 27, where they remain folded at the head of the cot. On the way back downstairs, he passes the man from the main activity room. The man stares, not sure if he recognized him in his street clothes.

He looks at his watch. It is 9:30.

He walks through the buzzing security door, runs down the stairs that open on to the street. He nearly collides with a prostitute who screams, "Holy shit! You could have given me a heart attack, running into me like that." He tries to apologize. A Black man, who has seen the whole thing, calls to her. "Leave the poor kid alone," he says, "he just needed some cooling off. Didn't you, Buddy? It gets awful steamy up there, doesn't it?"

THE WHITE ELEPHANT

On a warm, mid-1980's, mid-April Friday afternoon, Mrs. Simon, the woman from the realty office on Newbury Street, called Gordon at work. He wasn't at his desk when the call came, so Lisa took the message. Gordon's hands shook as he pushed the buttons on the phone, returning the call. He had committed the number to memory, hoping that it would bring him luck. Mrs. Simon answered on the first ring.

"The apartment on Marlborough Street is yours," she said. "Your references checked out just fine. You can pick up the keys any time this afternoon."

"Thank you for your help, Mrs. Simon," he said, trying to contain his excitement.

"Oh, you're welcome, young man. Congratulations and enjoy."

"Yee ha," Gordon hooted as soon as he hung up.

"You better call Robin," Lisa said, "he's been making excuses for coming here and hovering over your desk since I took the message."

Gordon dialed Robin's extension in the bookkeeping department. Robin answered on half a ring.

"Robin, I got the apartment."

"Yee ha," Robin said, "let's celebrate."

"I'm going to pick up the keys at lunch time," Gordon said, "we can buy some champagne or something and go to the apartment after work."

"I'll meet you at the elevator, 4:30 sharp," Robin said, and they hung up.

Gordon could hardly keep his mind on his work. The words on the loan applications in front of him seemed to swim on the paper. He was so excited, his heart pounded, and he wondered if anyone could see it through his sweater.

At lunchtime, he grabbed his jacket and headed for the stairs, too impatient to wait for the elevator. He ran down the stairs, two at a time, almost twisting his ankle on one of the landings. Out of the building, he ran down Boylston Street, turned on Clarendon and was at the Newbury Street realty office in a matter of minutes.

There were some formalities, papers to be signed. Gordon took the check out of his pocket that included the first month's rent, last month's rent and a finder's fee. He had been waiting for this moment for a long time and gladly handed over the check. Mrs. Simon shook his hand and gave him the keys. She also gave him a card with the landlord's phone number and the names and numbers of some maintenance men.

"Keep this by the phone," she said, "just in case."

He got a salad-to-go at the Salad Stop, next door to the realty office and checked his watch to see if he had time to take a quick run to the apartment. He had twenty minutes. That would give him just enough time to get to the building, stand in front of it admiringly and call it home.

When he got back to the office, he put the Styrofoam container filled with salad on his desk. There was a pale blue envelope leaning against his phone. He opened it. Inside, there was a card signed by Robin and Lisa. It said, "Best of luck in your new apartment." Gordon put it back in its envelope and stuck it in his jacket pocket.

He opened the Styrofoam salad-container and took a plastic knife and fork out of his desk drawer. There were onions on top of his salad, and he wondered if, in his hurry, he had forgotten to ask the salad preparer to leave them out.

Gordon and Robin walked to a liquor store on Boylston Street after work. Lisa had an appointment to get her hair cut and took a raincheck. Gordon bought a bottle of champagne and Robin bought a bottle of wine.

"The champagne is for the christening," Robin said, "the wine is for your first special occasion in your new home."

"Thank you," Gordon said, "we'll drink it when I have you over for dinner, as soon as I'm settled."

Gordon talked about his decorating plans, as they walked. He had living room furniture that his parents had been storing for him. It was some of the furniture they'd bought after they were married and in their first apartment. Some called it Fabulous Fifties or Mid-century Modern. Gordon had grown to appreciate it, now that it was back in vogue.

His parents helped him pay for the reupholstering of two oval, curved back chairs. The fabric had been green and faded. The wood on the arms and legs nicked, scratched. Now the wood was painted black and the fabric was black, too. There was a coffee table and a commode with two drawers.

Gordon remembered that his parents kept their wedding album in the second drawer of the commode when he was growing up. He wished that it had been part of the package, too. His parents had looked so young on their wedding day in 1957. His father still had hair. It was black and wavy. His mother's blonde hair had been shoulder-length and set with a curl.

Both the coffee table and the commode had matching burl wood parquet tops, and both were now painted a gun-metal grey. Gordon bought a lamp for the top of the commode. It was a black ginger jar with a grey shade. His brother and sister pitched in and bought him a black, folding futon sofa-bed. All the furniture was meant to replace what he had in the large studio apartment he had lived in, in the South End, for two years.

He had enjoyed the South End apartment, but not the neighborhood. It had become increasingly dangerous to walk the streets at night and even, sometimes, during the day. The studio was in a renovated building on Dartmouth Street and he paid a reasonable rent, for the area. He had moved home to his parents' house, in Randolph, after his apartment had been broken into and ransacked in the spring of 1983.

The burglars had taken his TV and VCR, his stereo and some of his jewelry. Among the jewelry was an old watch that had belonged to his grandfather. He had had it restored and it looked and worked like new. It was round, with a black face and gold numbers. As a child, he had often admired it and his grandfather had promised it to him. It had great sentimental value. Gordon offered a substantial reward for its return, but no one responded.

All the furniture had been hacked up. Stuffing from the sofa and pillows was everywhere. The detective who spoke to Gordon said they were probably looking for drugs. Before the building had been bought and gentrified, it had been a notorious hangout for pushers, dealers and junkies.

When the check from the insurance company arrived, Gordon put it into a high interest-bearing account at the bank where he worked. While it accrued interest, Gordon took his time looking for a new apartment. He looked at apartments outside of the city first, fed up with city living.

He looked in Brookline, Cambridge, Somerville, Allston-Brighton, Jamaica Plain, and even as far as Newton, Medford and Malden. He carefully checked each apartment and neighborhood to see how safe it was.

Since he didn't have his own car, commuting by mass transit was inevitable. He made sure the apartments he looked at were within walking distance of the nearest T station. He rode each train line and found the faults of each outweighed the merits. It had been so convenient living in the South End and walking to work.

With that in mind, he investigated the different Boston neighborhoods. The Symphony area was definitely out, as was the area around Boston University. The rents were high, and the apartments were nothing special. As for security, both neighborhoods were notorious for their high crime rates. He looked around the Fenway area and saw an apartment on Peterborough Street that he liked. But that neighborhood wasn't the safest either.

He looked in the Riverway but wasn't happy about the idea of riding the rickety, old Arborway trains to his office in Copley Square. The Riverway was out of the question.

Gordon also looked into the North End and the Waterfront. The rents were higher than he had anticipated, although the area was probably the safest to live in. The North End had a reputation for being self-policing and this appealed to Gordon. However, there were few apartments available, and the ones he saw, he didn't care for.

Beacon Hill was also out. He'd lived on the Hill as a student and recalled the tremendous cockroach problem he and his roommates had endured. Besides, the upper hill was out of his price range, and the lower hill was overrun with students and transients.

Gordon had always wanted to live in the Back Bay. So, he concentrated most of his efforts on that area. Robin lived in the Back Bay, on Beacon Street, and he was always trying to convince Gordon to move there.

In one week, Gordon spoke with half a dozen real estate agents until he met Mrs. Simon. She was a friendly older woman who spoke with a slight

German accent. She seemed genuinely concerned about Gordon's plight. In a matter of days, she'd shown him over a dozen apartments. Each had its own appeal, charm, but Gordon didn't feel "at home" in any of them.

Finally, when he'd just about given up, Mrs. Simon pulled a card out of her sleeve that she told Gordon she'd been "saving for someone like him." This puzzled him at first, but when he saw the apartment, he knew what she'd meant.

The apartment was on the third floor of a four-story building located in the middle of the block, between Dartmouth and Exeter streets, on the sunny side. It was a one-bedroom apartment, almost twice the size of Gordon's studio in the South End. There was a working fireplace and a wall of exposed brick. The kitchen was long and narrow.

Gordon and Mrs. Simon discussed the details of rent, maintenance, decorating and availability. It was agreed that he'd move in on the first of the month. This gave him a little over two weeks to get ready. He'd left a lot of things in boxes while staying at his parents' house. He walked Mrs. Simon back to the realty office and headed for home.

Robin and Gordon arrived at the building and Gordon unlocked the street door. They climbed the stairs. At the third floor, Gordon stopped and unlocked the door nearest the stairs.

"This is it," he said, "it needs a little work."

Gordon flicked a switch next to the door and the room was filled with light. There was a door with a full-length mirror to the right of the entrance. Gordon opened it to reveal a large walk-in closet. There were two horizontal poles on either side and six coat hooks on the back of the door.

Robin walked around the room. He stood in front of the stained-glass window on the wall that ran along the outside hall. Directly across from it was the wall with the fireplace. There was a semi-ornate mirror, built into the wall, over it. The floors were hardwood and had recently been refinished.

"Very spacious," Robin said. "The floor is beautiful. Better have your visitors leave their shoes outside."

The kitchen and bathroom were to the left of the front door. The streetlamps cast their peach-colored light on the kitchen floor. It was painted black and Gordon planned on putting down another coat before moving in.

Robin took the bottle of champagne out of the bag and started to laugh.

"What's so funny?" Gordon asked.

"No glasses," he said and popped the cork anyway.

It was 7:00. Gordon and Robin were both a little tipsy. They'd almost polished off the whole bottle of champagne, passing it back and forth between themselves. When they'd finished, Gordon suggested opening the bottle of wine.

"No," Robin said, "save it. Put it in the kitchen cupboard."

Gordon got up unsteadily from the floor where they'd been sitting. After he'd put the bottle of wine away, he stood in the doorway, between the kitchen and the living room.

"Let's go to Partners for a drink," he said.

Partners was a bar on Boylston Street, where they usually went to drink after work. After Massachusetts repealed Happy Hour, Partners had taken to serving hors d'oeuvres and having live entertainment before the hardcore crowd arrived. No matter, Partners was crowded from the time they opened their doors until after last call.

When Gordon and Robin got there, it was almost impossible to get to the bar. Someone called to them from a crowded table in a corner. Gordon found the source of the voice and discovered it was Curtis, Robin's ex-lover. With him were Mikhaila, Jeffery and Ted.

"Well, if it isn't Batman and Robin," Curtis said.

Curtis and Robin had been lovers for a short time during the summer before. Curtis still harbored some love for Robin, but Robin wanted little to do with him. Curtis had a serious substance abuse problem. Robin had called it quits, saying he was tired of having to carry Curtis out of Partners at closing time.

Gordon leaned over and kissed Curtis on the cheek.

"Curt as ever, Curtis," he said.

Curtis frowned at Robin, who was looking around the bar.

"It's your turn, Robin," Curtis said, offering the same cheek. Robin brushed his cheek against Curtis's.

"Air kisses, how rich," Curtis said.

The others at the table were doing their best to look comfortable, hoping Curtis wouldn't turn and attack one of them. It was still early, and Curtis was pretty far gone. He must have started drinking at lunch, Gordon thought.

"Where have you guys been?" Mikhaila, the only woman at the table, asked.

"I was showing Robin my new apartment," Gordon said, "I got the keys this afternoon and I can move in any time."

"Where are you moving to?" Jeffery, Curtis' current love interest, asked.

"Marlborough Street, between Dartmouth and Exeter," Gordon answered.

"Deserting the Valley of the Dolls?" Curtis asked. "I thought you liked it there."

"I did, until my apartment was broken into."

"That's right," Mikhaila said, "I remember Robin mentioning that."

"It was pretty devastating. They wrecked my furniture, took my stereo and some jewelry."

"Oh, we aren't going to have to listen to that story about that damn watch again, are we?" Curtis said, hurtfully.

"No, Curtis," Gordon said, "I wouldn't want to bore you with stories that have any emotional impact."

The comedian who had been performing at Partners for a few weeks was getting ready to go on. The room began to quiet. Gordon excused himself from the group at the table and went into the men's room. The men's room was almost as crowded as the rest of the bar. He saw a couple of people he knew and exchanged hellos. Two of the men were talking about a friend of theirs who had been hospitalized, something that was becoming a typical mid-1980s conversation.

"He looks terrible," one of them said, "you wouldn't even recognize him."

"He liked to live fast," the other said, "I hope he goes fast. I can't stand the thought of him suffering."

"His parents won't go see him in the hospital. Mickey and I sent him flowers. Some of us are getting together and going to see him. You can come too, if you want."

"Tomorrow's Saturday and I've got some errands to run in the morning. How about early afternoon?"

"That sounds fine," the tall one with red hair said. "I'll pick you up around 12:45."

While Gordon was washing his hands, he remembered that the Morgan Memorial Goodwill store on Berkley was having a used furniture sale. He decided to ask Robin if he wanted to go shopping with him. He was looking for a coat rack and a free-standing floor lamp. In keeping with his fabulous fifties decorating motif, he thought Morgie's might be the place to start.

When he walked out of the bathroom, he saw that blonde kid who had bought him a drink the night before. He was a grad student at Boston University. His name was Perry, and he lived off-campus, near the Fenway. They had talked for quite a while in a quiet corner of the bar. Just as Gordon was getting ready to invite him back to his apartment, to see him naked by candlelight, he remembered that he didn't have his own place yet, and that bringing Perry home to Randolph was out of the question. So, they said goodnight and parted ways.

"Perry? Hi, it's Gordon," Gordon said, tapping him on the shoulder of his blue Oxford cloth shirt.

"Hey, Gordon, how's it going?"

"Better," Gordon said, reaching into his pocket and producing the new keys to his flat. "I found a new apartment...in the neighborhood."

"That's great. You all moved in?"

"No, I just signed the lease and took possession today. You'll have to come by when there's a place to sit."

"Yeah," Perry said, "or recline."

"That'd be nice, too," Gordon said, weighing the options of taking Perry to the empty Marlborough Street apartment now, making love to him on the hardwood floor by the light of the streetlamps. He did have a bottle of wine there, after all.

"Here's my number," Perry said, busily scribbling away on a soggy cocktail napkin. The blue ink blurred a little but was still legible.

"Call me soon," Perry said and kissed Gordon on the ear.

When Gordon returned to the table, Robin was the only one still sitting there.

"I thought you'd abandoned me," Robin said.

"Where'd everybody go?"

"Home to nap. Resting up for a rendezvous at the Pigeonhole, later. You up for it?"

The Pigeonhole was an after-hours bar that Gordon had been to a few times. He considered a walk on the wilder side for a moment. He still had some energy but thought it best to go home to his parents' house and sleep, so he could be up early for a Saturday shopping spree.

"No, I don't think so. I was hoping to do some shopping tomorrow. Would you like to accompany me?"

Robin looked at his watch and yawned.

"If you weren't planning on getting started too early, yes. I'll just go home and get some shut eye. Call me before you leave the house. That should give me enough time to primp."

Gordon and Robin left Partners together. They said good night on the corner of Berkeley and Boylston. Robin headed for Beacon Street and Gordon walked towards the Back Bay commuter rail station.

Spring was evident in the buds on the trees and the couples and groups walking down Boylston street with or without lightweight jackets or sweatshirts. Gordon had weathered a stormy fall and winter in the suburbs and was getting ready to bloom again, in the city.

Gordon and Robin were having breakfast at Division Sixteen. While Robin buttered and spread marmalade on his toast, Gordon fished in his pocket for his list.

"Here it is," Gordon said, unfolding the piece of yellow legal pad paper.

"What's the first stop?" Robin asked, crunching whole wheat toast.

"There are a couple of antique stores I wanted to check out. Three on Charles Street and one on Tremont. Since we're closer to the South End, let's hit Tremont Street first. We can stop at Morgan Memorial on the way."

"You really are serious about Morgie's, aren't you? You know, you aren't a college student anymore. You can afford to buy real furniture."

"I know," Gordon said, picking at his omelet. "I just don't want to miss any spectacular finds. You never know what's going to turn up at the Goodwill."

"Or crawl out," Robin said. "The last time I was there, with Mikhaila, we watched a family of mice do a kick-line in the middle of the floor."

"I'm not worried about that. I keep hoping to find that elusive fabulous fifties treasure that will complement the rest of my decor."

"Well, flag down the waitress and get the check. From the looks of your list, we're going to need all day."

Saturday traffic crawled slowly up Boylston Street. The nice weather seemed to be here to stay, for a little while, at least. Robin took in the sights from the passenger's side. Gordon absentmindedly changed channels on the car's radio. He turned right on Clarendon and drove past police headquarters.

"Did you talk to anyone who went to Pigeonhole last night? Did they get raided again?"

"No, on both counts," Robin said. "I keep having this nightmare that I'm there during a raid. In the dream, my mother is chief of the vice squad. Everyone has their pants down around their ankles, except me. My mother says, 'Okay boys, this is a raid. You all have to go home and call your mothers.' And then she points at me and says, 'Arrest him.' I usually wake up with the top sheet twisted around my wrists like a pair of handcuffs."

"You have to admit, operating an after-hours sex club around the corner from police headquarters is pretty daring," Gordon said.

"It just makes it easier when the time comes to pay them off. They're getting pretty good at looking the other way," Robin joked.

"Did you see the interview with that woman in *Gay Boston*," Gordon asked, "the one we saw standing by the Pigeonhole entrance last time we were there handing out condoms? I think she calls herself 'Saint Moan.'"

"Yeah, she's there every Friday and Saturday night."

Gordon pulled his father's car into a parking space across the street from the Morgan Memorial Goodwill store.

"Remember your list, Gordon. There are lots of other places to get to before sundown. I wouldn't want you to miss out on anything because we spent too much time at Morgie's," Robin said, smiling.

"Don't worry. I promise not to linger too long among the rodent infestation. At the first sign of city wildlife, we'll leave."

"Well," Robin said, "I'm going to stay upstairs and try to put together my new spring wardrobe. If you find anything in the furniture dungeon and you need a second opinion, just ask."

The store was in full swing and appeared to be bursting at the seams with newly arrived old merchandise. Sleepy-looking girls in blue smocks sorted through bags and boxes of used clothes, puncturing them with needle-tipped price tag guns. The shoppers were from all walks of life; young, old, black, white, trendy, and poor. Gordon walked down the cracked concrete stairs to the basement, where tables and chairs were arranged in a helter-skelter fashion.

He saw a kitchen table with a marbleized Formica top and chrome legs and trim, but there was only one matching chair, the vinyl upholstery glittering and slashed. There was a loveseat balanced on three legs. As he walked, he glanced at the floor for mouse droppings or the sight of a long skinny tail disappearing under a recliner or a davenport.

He was ready to agree with Robin, rummage through the shelves of dog-eared paperbacks before going back upstairs, when he saw it. It stood against a wall, under a stack of quilts and comforters.

For a moment, Gordon stood where he was, a few feet away from it, transfixed. He heard two women, conversing in Spanish, come up behind him. They kept walking past him, one on either side, and stopped right in front of it, blocking his view. One of the women, the shorter of the two, began rifling through the stack of blankets and throws. She pulled out an afghan, done in oranges and browns, that unfolded, and she had to hold her arms high up over her head so that it wouldn't touch the ground.

Her companion grabbed the bottom and they stretched it out between them. They inspected the afghan, turning it over a few times, before coming together to fold it in half, and then fold it again. The taller one flung the folded afghan over her shoulder and they moved on.

Gordon moved forward, one hand outstretched, in something of a trance, and touched the wood of the hi-fi. He moved his hand across it slowly until he reached the raised plastic letters. He crouched and touched the word Zenith, the Z like a lightning bolt, underlining the rest of the letters. He put both hands on the mesh-fabric front, feeling it give slightly at his touch. He could feel the woofer and tweeter underneath.

He closed his eyes. He saw the same hi-fi standing in the living room of his parents' house, the house where he grew up. His father loved jazz and his mother loved show-tunes and John Gary. Gordon's love of music began and ended with recorded music. He couldn't read a note, and since the time his voice had changed during adolescence, he restricted his singing to the shower and the car with the windows rolled up.

As a child, he had loved to sing. The bigger the audience, the better. His mother would put a record on the turntable of the hi-fi and Gordon would sing along with Petula Clark or Doris Day or Andy Williams. He did this at birthday parties, holiday and family gatherings. He liked singing to songs by girls best, his high child's voice matching the singer note for note. The words to the songs that the ladies sang sounded better to him, too. He was only five or six, but he was already beginning to understand heartbreak and how cruel men could be.

Gordon got his own phonograph when he was four, but the records sounded different, not as good as they did on the big Zenith hi-fi in the living room. He would take his phonograph, which had a lid with a latch and handle for easy transporting, into the living room and ask his mother to plug it in for him. Then he would lift the lid and put miniature farm animals, little green plastic soldiers posed in various positions of combat, and brown plastic cowboys and Indians on the turntable. He would set the speed at 16 or 33 RPM's, because he had learned through experience, running around his room picking up the scattered miniatures, that 45 or 78 was much too fast, and he would turn the phonograph on, the turntable spinning slow enough not to make his toys dizzy or launch them into flight.

He had also learned how to operate the Zenith, and he would put a record on, something by Perry Como or Allan Sherman, and he would sing along, moving his feet, his little body swaying from side to side, and pretend he was on the *Ed Sullivan Show* or *American Bandstand*.

Gordon was humming to himself when he felt a hand on his shoulder.

"I'm sorry, sir, but that's been sold."

He stood up quickly, feeling a little lightheaded, and was face to face with Robin, who was laughing.

"See?" he said and pointed to the yellow tag with the red writing hanging from a piece of string taped to a corner of the hi-fi.

Gordon touched the tag, turned it over and read the price on the other side. It said, $15.00.

"I'll offer them thirty for it."

"This isn't exactly an open-air market," Robin said, "I don't know how they feel about haggling. Although I'm sure you'd be the first person to offer them more money for something in the store."

"It's mine. I have to have it."

"You don't even know if it works."

"If it doesn't work," Gordon said, "I'll have it fixed, or use it as a planter."

"It'll probably ruin your records. And I don't think it plays cassettes or CDs. I don't even think it plays 8-track tapes."

"Robin, this is exactly what I've been looking for. We had one just like this when I was a kid. In fact, this just might have been ours."

"If so, it must have been sitting down here a long time. Unless, your parents recently remodeled."

"I have to find a salesclerk," Gordon said, heading for the stairs.

"Wait for me," Robin said, "I don't want to get rabies or tetanus down here."

Gordon walked over to one of the cashiers, who was absentmindedly playing with her hair while a heavyset black woman unloaded a shopping cart full of caftans onto the counter.

"Excuse me," Gordon said, "there's a piece of furniture downstairs, marked sold, that I was interested in buying."

"If it's been *mocked* sold," the cashier said, inspecting her split ends, "it's *awready* been bought."

"But, if it's still down there..."

"Well, maybe *whoeva* bought it couldn't take it with them. Maybe *theah comin'* back *faw* it today."

"It's marked $15.00. I'll offer you thirty."

"You can *offa* me all you want, *sih*. If it's *mocked* sold, it's sold."

"Where's the manager?" Gordon asked, losing his patience with the girl, who's Dorchester accent was beginning to work his nerves.

"At the *customa sehvice* desk. Now, if you'll excuse me, I have *otha customas* to take *ca'e* of."

The cashier dismissed him with her back and Gordon felt his anger rise. He was just about to say something to her, when Robin led him away, towards the counter with the Customer Service sign hanging over it.

"Gordon, old friend," Robin said in a tone of voice meant to calm, "it will do you no good to argue with Miss O'Brien. Give her a break. Cashiering at Morgie's is a step up from flipping burgers at Mickey D's. Don't try to get her fired, okay?"

"I'm not going to get her fired. I just want to close her fingers in her cash drawer."

Gordon didn't have much luck with the store manager either. The woman who bought the hi-fi had left a three dollar down payment on it and was coming back some time that afternoon with the rest of the money. The store policy said something about holding merchandise for 30 days if a deposit was left.

"You mean to tell me that she only put three dollars down, and you're going to hold it for her until she comes up with the other twelve dollars?"

"That's right, sir," the manager said. He was a kid, probably in his mid-twenties, with brown hair and acne scars.

"When was she here?"

"Yesterday, sir."

"Yesterday?" Gordon repeated, as if he needed clarification. "You're sure she said she'd be back with the rest of the money today?"

"Actually, I'm not sure. Miss O'Brien took the deposit from her."

Gordon turned around to look back at the cashier. She was talking into a microphone near her cash register, asking for a price check, her mouth too close to it to be understood.

"Excuse me," the manager said, in the same fake polite way that Miss O'Brien had used, "but I need to get a price for Miss O'Brien."

"Wait a second," Gordon felt himself beginning to plead, "what if I offer you thirty dollars? What if I offer to take it with me today?"

"I'm sorry, sir, I can't do that. Store policy. You understand, don't you? Now, if you'll excuse me..."

Before Gordon could respond, the store manager walked away. He looked at Robin, who had stood by silently.

"Revenge is yours," Robin said, "just wait till he tries to come to you for a loan."

That night, Gordon's sleep was populated with dreams. He dreamed that Miss O'Brien invited him and Perry, the B.U. student from Partners, over for dinner. When they arrived at her house in Dorchester, there was a small table set with four chairs. The store manager was sitting in one of them and he motioned for Gordon and Perry to sit down. Gordon tried to pull his chair in closer to the table, but he couldn't, something was blocking him, and he had to sit with his legs to one side. The table was low and covered with a stained, lace tablecloth, that the manager pointed out was purchased at Morgie's. Through the lace, Gordon could make out the surface of the table. It was the same color wood as the hi-fi. Miss O'Brien came out of the kitchen, carrying a silver tray with a lid on it. She put it in the center of the table, the edges of the tray hanging over the top. She lifted the lid to reveal four Big Macs in their Styrofoam containers. Gordon suddenly stood up and grabbed a handful of the tablecloth. He yanked it, like he'd seen so many magicians do over the years. Everything went flying, and underneath was the hi-fi.

Gordon woke up with a start.

He thought he'd sworn Robin to secrecy. He was wrong. He thought Robin would think twice before telling anyone about the scene he'd made at the Goodwill store. Wrong, again.

"How's the great Victrola hunt going?" Lisa asked him, as they rode up to their office in the elevator.

"How did you...it's not a Victrola, it's a hi-fi. Boy, Robin couldn't wait until today to tell you? He had to call you at home over the weekend?"

"Gordon, he told me about what happened. He was freaked, he'd never seen you like that before. By the way, does it have a simulated wood cabinet?"

"I guess you'll just have to wait until it's delivered to my apartment to see, now, won't you?"

"Morgie's delivers?"

"They will after the call I'm going to make to the headquarters of Goodwill Industries."

"Maybe you should make the call from Robin's office. That way you can close the door, and no one will be able to hear you screaming."

Gordon's phone call to Goodwill's home office proved to be as disastrous and unfruitful as his visit to the Morgan Memorial. They seemed to be more interested in adhering to rules than to pleasing customers. Gordon thought that Miss O'Brien and the store manager had a great future with the organization. Gordon was not about to give up.

Beginning at 10:00, when the store opened, Gordon began calling every hour to ask if the mysterious $3.00-down-payment-woman had surfaced to claim her prize. He started to feel like one of two people who had just won the Megabucks Lottery and he had to wait until the other one appeared with their ticket to find out whether he had to share his winnings or if he could keep them all to himself.

This went on for a week. His pursuit of the hi-fi was ceaseless. He had a phone installed in his new apartment, so he could call Morgie's while he painted or put up bookshelves or finished getting the apartment ready for when his furniture and other belongings would arrive on the moving van in less than a week. A couple of nights, he slept on the living room floor in a sleeping bag.

Perry had called once, and asked Gordon if he wanted to meet for drinks at Partners. It was a Thursday night and Morgie's was open until 9:00. Gordon didn't want to leave the apartment on the off chance that he might miss out on preventing the hi-fi from leaving the store.

There were still two weeks left to the thirty days since the deposit on the Zenith was made. Gordon was putting the finishing touches on the apartment, then going to his parents' house to organize the boxes of his stuff and his furniture for the move. In his mind, he could see where everything would go in the new apartment. He even left room, against a wall, for the hi-fi. He didn't possess it yet, but he knew he would.

The night before his move, he was in the basement of his parents' house, putting the clothes he had left in his closet into a packing box. He was getting used to the loud sound the packing tape made when it was peeled off the roll. His mother came downstairs with a cup of tea.

"You look tired," she said, "have some tea."

"Thanks," he said, and blew steam off the top before sipping it.

"By this time tomorrow," his mother said, "you'll be all moved into your new place. It was really nice having you back, for the short time that you were here."

Gordon smiled. Living at home again, after having moved out, wasn't as bad as he'd anticipated. He got along better with his father than he had before he'd moved out the first time. It was nice, too, having other people, a family, to sit down to dinner with. Now that he'd be living on his own again, he'd have to be the cook and the maid and the laundry person.

"Thanks, Mom. I really owe you and Dad a debt of gratitude for taking me in after my catastrophe. Once I'm all settled in, I'll have you both over for dinner. How does that sound?"

"It sounds great. Listen, I was going through some stuff down here, the other day, and I found a box of old comic books. I think you left them here after your first move. If you have a chance, look through them, because I was thinking of giving them away."

"Sure," Gordon said, "where are they?"

"Over there," his mother pointed to a stack of boxes, near some antique chairs she had bought at a yard sale and his father had promised to refinish and reupholster.

"I'm going to get ready for bed," his mother said, "don't stay up too late. You have to be up early tomorrow morning."

"I won't," he said, and then he kissed her on the cheek. "Good night, Mom, and thanks again."

"Don't mention it," she said, "it was our pleasure."

His mother went upstairs, and Gordon drained the cup. He put the cup and saucer on top of the clothes dryer. He yawned and stretched and looked at his watch. It was getting late. He quickly inspected the boxes he had just packed to make sure they were tightly sealed. He was getting ready to call it a night, when he remembered the box of comic books. He considered waiting until morning, but he knew that things would be too hectic with the movers and all. He was glad he went to the box, marked "comix," because underneath it was the old Zenith hi-fi he remembered so vividly from his childhood.

MONEY CHANGING
HANDS

$

When you tell people that you work as a teller, at a bank in downtown Boston, they usually have one of two reactions. The ones your age ask you if it makes you nervous, handling all that money. Do you ever think about helping yourself to any of it? they ask. What happens if your drawer is short at the end of the day? What's the combination to the vault?

The older ones, the professionals, look at you funny, as if your nose were bleeding or your lower eyelid was twitching in code. You have a pierced ear, they say. You wear ten black rubber O-ring bracelets on your wrist, like Madonna, they say. You have a new-wave haircut, complete with close shaved sides and a skinny, braided tail, they say. Shouldn't you be waiting tables at Quincy Market or singing for change in the T station, they ask?

$ $

On your first day on the job at a bank in Kendall Square, a job you held on to for two excruciating months in 1984, one of the indistinguishable Cambridge women that you worked with pointed out ground zero to you. Draper Labs, she said, pointing through the double-paned, bulletproof glass of the drive-up teller's window. And over there, she motioned in the general vicinity of over there, M.I.T. They ever drop the bomb, she says, they'll drop it there first. They ever drop the bomb, she says, we're ash.

On the day that you interviewed for this other job at this other bank near Downtown Crossing, you left early from the job you hated at the bank in Kendall Square. I have a doctor's appointment, you said to the dyspeptic branch manager that morning. I must have my head examined for ever taking this job, you said to no one in particular, as you boarded the bus that took you over the Longfellow Bridge into Boston for the interview.

$ $ $

The vice president of the bank in Boston, a middle-aged woman with the blackest hair you have ever seen on someone not Asian, interviews you with a curious mixture of genuine interest and outright indifference. There are framed photographs of two black teacup poodles with red ribbons clipped to their ears on her desk. You can't help but wonder if she dyes her hair black to match the dogs' fur.

$ $ $ $

Much to your delight, all three of the tellers on the all-male teller line of the Boston bank are gay. You are the fourth. Now you can all play bridge.
Over time, you learn that two of the bank's loan officers are also gay, as is the older man in bookkeeping. There is a closeted customer service rep, who is convinced that no one knows he is gay. Even the president of the bank, a former Jesuit priest, has been known to eat forbidden fruit.

After the bank's Christmas party, you go, with the other tellers, to a charming piano bar, around the corner from the swank hotel where the party is being held. You are all dressed up, having come right from the party, and you discover that this is where all the other tellers from all the other downtown banks have come after their Christmas parties have ended. When you tell a teller from a bank on Franklin Street where you work, he throws his head back and laughs, like an actress. Oh, he says, you work at the gay bank.

$ $ $ $ $

The decor of the bank is colonial. Early-American-blue walls, blue carpeting, wood trim painted white. Brass wall sconces and chandeliers illuminate the intimate lobby. It's a historical building, safe from unsightly, protective Plexiglas at the teller windows.

$ $ $ $ $

Money changes hands, from the teller to the robber. No time to set off the silent alarm. No time for a password. Time both stands perfectly still and jerks forward. You look at your hands as if they have come unattached from your body. They are the hands of a grave-digger, a concert pianist, a nail-biter. They are as unsteady as a newborn animal, as defined as the hands in an Escher drawing. You are sure they will be useless after this. You will never write another poem, slide another record album out of its sleeve, button another shirt, masturbate, again.

$ $ $ $ $ $

He is stuffing the money into the pockets of his black leather jacket. "Okay," he says, "that's enough." He smiles, showing a gold tooth. He smells as if he stopped at the fragrance counter in Filene's on the way to the bank and was accosted by dozens of cologne spraying clerks. He winks.

$ $ $ $ $ $ $

No witnesses. The other tellers are pre-occupied. Playing cards, filing their nails, doing crossword puzzles, reading romance novels. You suddenly realize that you have never been adequately prepared for a moment such as this one. You rely on your wits, which are vibrating like microwaves one minute, fraying like a shoelace the next.

When it's over, you wonder if you will be able to describe this man, this event, and do it justice. You focus on how alone you felt, even though you weren't. The sound of your breathing in your ears, making it hard for you to understand the bank robber's instructions, as if he were giving you directions through two enormous seashells connected by a strand of pearls. What about eye contact? With the head-teller? The mask-less robber? His accomplices, standing guard in the bank's lobby while eating soft, mustard coated pretzels?

You worry that he won't be satisfied with all the money from your drawer. What if he asks you to empty your own pockets onto the counter? You imagine that everything of value in your pockets will be reduced to small change, a cat's eye marble, penny candy wrappers, a yo-yo, a ticket stub, a comb, the orthodontic retainer you were certain you had lost in a movie theater years before. Your sleeves have crept up over your wrists, exposing your favorite wristwatch, the one your parents gave you for your twenty-fifth birthday, and you wonder if you are willing to die for it, for anything at all.

$ $ $ $ $ $ $ $

When it's over, you stand over your reflection in a toilet. Somehow you imagined yourself vomiting pennies.

$ $ $ $ $ $ $ $ $

At home, the night of the hold-up, your eyelids are heavy as half-dollars. Your lover comes home from the office with flowers that he bought from a street vendor. He is not sure if this is the appropriate gift for someone who has faced his own mortality. The smell of the flowers makes you alternately nauseous and ravenous.

You try napping, but the hold-up replays itself repeatedly inside your eyelids as if they were giant drive-in movie screens. Your lover crawls into bed beside you, tries rocking you to sleep in his arms, then suggests that he suck you off, not sure if this is the suitable offer to make someone who has faced his own mortality.

There is a knock at the front door, and you are visibly startled, convinced that the bank robber and his cohorts have come to dispose of you. Or maybe it is one of the detectives that you spoke to after the robbery. The one you thought was sexy-in-a-law-enforcement-officer-kind-of-way, coming by to make sure that you are all right, safe, being looked after. You don't verbalize either of these thoughts, certain that your lover will think you are either paranoid or cheating on him.

It is neither the bank robber nor the detective, but Dan, a neighbor. Your lover called him right after he hung up with you, right after you told him about what had happened at the bank. Dan reaches into his shirt pocket and pulls out a long, fat joint, rolled in rolling paper that is printed to look like currency.

Dan and your lover are always getting stoned together. You haven't gotten high for awhile, maybe a year, and while it seems appealing now, you decline. Well, there's more where this came from, Dan says, friendly as a neighborhood drug dealer.

Within minutes the joint is a roach. Then they are hungry. You're not sure if it's a contact high or the hour, six o'clock, but you are hungry too, and grateful that your appetite has returned, the earlier nausea subsided.

The three of you walk from your street on Beacon Hill to a seafood restaurant on the waterfront. You are glad that it is summer, and that you can still get away with wearing sunglasses at this hour. You changed clothes three times before leaving the house, not wanting to wear anything that would call attention to yourself, not realizing that three gay men, giggling and cruising while walking through the North End in the early 1980s, was automatically a reason to stare.

After dinner, you and your lover go back to Dan's apartment, across the street from your own apartment, where you finally relent, and join them in the third joint of the evening (they smoked the second one on the walk from the restaurant back to Beacon Hill).

In much the same way that you have trouble recalling the specific events of the hold-up -- What were his exact words? the sexy-in-a-law-enforcement-officer-kind-of-way detective had asked you. You told him that you didn't remember; that the gun pointed at your chest had confused you – it is a blur as to how you and your lover and Dan ended up in Dan's bed together. Was it the pot? Your weakened and defenseless state of being?

You and your lover have been together for a couple of years, and you have somehow managed to keep the sex interesting, varied. You are not sure if this three-way was planned or spontaneous. Was it your lover who wanted to get Dan into bed or vice versa? In your mind, you don't even figure into the equation.

When your lover reaches between Dan's legs, he subtly brushes his hand away. When he puts his hand on your stomach, Dan slaps his hand. It is then that it becomes clear to you that Dan has engineered this, that it is you he is interested in, and your lover gets out of the bed to fire up another joint and observe the action from the doorway of the bedroom, and you feel sad. You extend a hand to him, as if you were drowning in quicksand, and he had the power to rescue you or be pulled under with you, but he just turns away. You hear him in the kitchen, and imagine that he is standing, naked, in front of the open door of Dan's refrigerator, the stoned and scorned man's equivalent of a cold shower.

$ $ $ $ $ $ $ $ $ $

For weeks you dream about a man with a gold tooth, standing at your refrigerator, eating lettuce. You give up greens, start eating meat again. You feel better than you have in years.

For weeks, you think you see him everywhere. In a stretch limousine, on the subway, on the street. You are sure you saw him selling "sense" in the Common. You consider shaving your head, wearing a hat, spending a lot of time at a tanning salon. When a friend who hadn't heard about the hold-up gets angry because you ignored him when he called out to you in front of the old State House, you wonder if it's worth losing his friendship or telling the story for the millionth time.

Everyday you take a new route home. You feel better than you have in years.

$ $ $ $ $ $ $ $ $ $ $

Your co-workers make you a hero. One of them suggests a parade in your honor. You will sit in the back of a convertible, waving a white-gloved hand. Money falls from the sky like confetti.

$ $ $ $ $ $ $ $ $ $ $ $

It doesn't take long for you to realize that the only ones who understand you are other bank tellers who have also been victims of a hold-up. You think it would be a good idea to form a support group. The sense of violation that you feel is akin to losing a vital organ. You wonder if this is the bank teller's equivalent of rape.

After a few weeks, you jump less when the front door of the bank squeaks open and a customer enters. You still eye the vestibule suspiciously, like the old man looking out his window, waiting to yell at the neighborhood children playing on his overgrown front lawn. However, air doesn't catch in your lungs – half-hiccup, half-heartbeat – and you get back to the business of deposits and withdrawals. You keep the cash in your drawer low, make frequent visits to the vault.

$ $ $ $ $ $ $ $ $ $ $ $

Six months later, another bank robber sidles up to your window. This time, you're ready.

6TH & E

It began with a whistle. Two notes. One high, one low. The kind of whistle construction workers at a construction site blow at passing women showing even the most negligible amount of skin. The kind of whistle an amateur birdwatcher might attempt to get the attention of a bird high up in a tree. All I know is that it got my attention.

At the time, I was living on Capitol Hill. On E Street, between 6th & 7th, Northeast. The townhouse, which was in the middle of the block, was owned by two friends of my lover Milo. Bob was a former teacher of Milo's, Jack a former classmate. I rented the only finished room; second floor, center of the house, to the right at the top of the stairs.

Bob and Jack had bought the house in 1986, a year before the summer I moved in. They were in the process of slowly remodeling it. Jack had a booming interior design firm in the neighborhood, walking distance from the house. Bob taught at one of the local universities. I moved in with them when the house in which I had been living in Mount Pleasant became uninhabitable.

In August, when Milo and some of our friends helped me move in, we had been dating for a little over a year. During that time, we never actually lived together, although the subject arose many times. While he was working and residing in Washington, Milo lived six blocks from Jack and Bob's house. By the time I moved in, he had already left town. Milo had moved to Baltimore in June, to go to graduate school at Johns Hopkins, in a program that was not offered in any of Washington D.C.'s fine institutions of higher learning.

At the time, we had talked about me moving to Baltimore with him. It reminded me of Boston, where I grew up, before my family moved to Bethesda, Maryland. It was on the water, it had history. But I was in the process of quitting graduate school. I had a job that I hated as much as I loved. My parents were begging me to move back home, stop paying high rent in Mount Pleasant, where I had been living with a neurotic woman, her sister and their three cats.

I wanted to write. To be with Milo, and to write. I was working as a receptionist at Bouffant Circle, the hippest hair salon in DuPont Circle. I sat in the window, looking bored, making appointments for boring people from all over the Washington metropolitan area. I thought I would have plenty to write about after spending my days looking out onto Connecticut Avenue, watching the parade of pathos. But I longed to be in school.

When I got to class and listened to another endless lecture on the importance of neo-formalism in late twentieth-century poetry, I wished I was back at Bouffant Circle, filling in the appointment book in #2 pencil and gossiping with the clients and stylists.

Milo and I talked on the phone every day. I loved him more than I'd ever loved anyone else. He was very supportive of my writing and encouraged me all the time. Whenever I had a poem published in some small college literary journal, he would buy three or four copies and give them as gifts. He would subscribe to them to "keep them alive" as he said, so I could publish in them again and again.

Milo believed in me more than I had ever believed in myself. There was complete trust in our relationship. I believed in absolute monogamy, total commitment to one person and he said he felt the same way. Neither of us had been promiscuous before we met and with the health crisis being what it was, we vowed to be true to each other. And we were.

Until the man in the first-floor apartment on the corner of 6th & E, Northeast, whistled at me. I was walking home from the Metro stop at Union Station and was waiting for the stoplight on the corner to turn green. The batteries on my Walkman had died on the subway, but I left the headphones on anyway. It discouraged strangers from talking to me, asking for money or directions to the Smithsonian.

Traffic was unusually heavy, and I actually had to wait for the green light. While I was standing there, I heard someone whistle. It was coming from behind me and I considered turning around to look at the source. But then I remembered that I was still wearing the headphones and in keeping with my policy of ignoring the world around me, I stared straight ahead.

When the light turned green and I could cross, I stood on the corner, not moving, for about ten seconds, to see if anyone had come up behind me who looked like a whistler or a whistlee. I was the only one there, on that corner, at 6:00 that Tuesday evening. I crossed the street as the Don't Walk sign started to blink.

He whistled again on Wednesday, Thursday and Friday. I say he, because I saw him, or part of him. It was nearing the end of a summer I spent working full time at Bouffant Circle, while I pondered what to do about my future. My schedule almost never varied. I was on the corner of 6th and E by 6:00 every weeknight. The salon was closed on Mondays and I started earlier on Saturday and was home by 3:30. Neither of us was around much on weekends, but you could set a clock by him Tuesday through Friday.

The whistler lived on the first floor of a three-story apartment building, on the northeast corner of 6th & E. From the street, I could see most of the rooms and corresponding windows. Facing onto E Street was a small, high up kitchen window, the closest to the apartment building entrance. Next to that was his living room. His windows were always open, although he kept the mini-blinds half-drawn, when he was at home. A sofa or love seat was flush against that windowed wall. Directly opposite the window was a fireplace with a large mantle, painted white. I could see the blue lights on his receiver, a CD player and cassette deck. I could tell from the glow that it cast, that the TV was on a stand in front of the fireplace.

As one week bled into the next, I grew to anticipate his evening salutation. I would make sure my flat top was standing evenly, that the laces on my white leather Adidas high tops were tied. I wore baggy shorts and printed, over-sized t-shirts to work. That mid-'80s summer Tammy Faye Bakker, Pee Wee Herman, dinosaurs and a punk rock Gumby, among other images were silk-screened across my chest. I had just quit smoking at the beginning of the summer and was conscious of a slight weight gain on my usually thin frame. I thought the walk to and from the Metro station was good exercise.

By the end of the second week, I was in a quandary. Milo had been in summer school since the beginning of summer. When he wasn't doing research or writing a paper, he drove down to D.C. to spend time with me. On most Saturday nights, however, I would take Amtrak to Baltimore. It was convenient, since Union Station serviced Amtrak as well as Metro.

I'd stay with him in the graduate dorm, where we had wildly safe sex and ordered pizzas and Chinese food. Occasionally, we'd head out, go dancing at the Hippo or meet friends at a seedy bar in Fells Point or have dinner at his favorite crab house near the Inner Harbor. He had arranged his schedule so that he didn't have classes on Monday, my day off, so we could have a full weekend together. Occasionally, he'd call me at work on Saturday and tell me he was too bogged down for a visit. I'd leave work, carrying my weekend bag, filled with condoms, water-based lube and other accoutrements, back to the house, where it would sit in a corner of my room, still packed until Monday night. I was always afraid that if I unpacked it on Saturday, I'd end up crying myself to sleep.

The weekends with Milo were something to look forward to; a reward for getting through the week in one piece. Having a man whistling at me from his apartment window didn't make life any easier. In fact, the complications that existed, coupled with my growing curiosity, were a potentially lethal combination.

At first, when it all began, I considered telling my housemate Bob. To me, he was older and wise beyond his years. He had been out almost as long as I'd been alive. He was a well-known figure in gay Washington. An outspoken activist, a well-respected educator, cherished as a friend and confidant, I felt very close to him. He opened the doors of his house to me at a time when I thought I'd never find a place to live. But as close as he was to me, he was that much closer to Milo. I couldn't risk telling him for fear he would misunderstand and confuse matters even more.

I added the whistler to my growing list of traumas. My advisor at school advised me to make up my mind about my plans for the fall term and be quick about it. There were a few too many incoming grad students and if I didn't want to return to classes I had to let him know soon. Time was running out. In addition to that, just as I'd gotten settled into Jack and Bob's house, my parents started in again about me moving back home. My room was as I left it, they reminded me. No rules this time, they insisted, I could come and go as I pleased. How, I wondered, could I come and go as I pleased, if either action involved asking my parents for the keys to the car. Their house was nowhere near a Metro station, and a ridiculously long walk to the closest bus stop.

Then there was Milo. If I moved to Baltimore and we got a place together, how long would it last? Neither of us had lived with a lover before and we were both apprehensive. Milo was something of a slob. When he was still living on Capitol Hill, he and his gay-Republican roommate lived in what we all comically referred to as the "slaughterhouse." They both worked long hours and were busy with social activities outside of the house. Patrick went to his political rallies, which I insisted were Hitler Youth assemblies. Milo and I plunged into a very concentrated romance. Love at first sight and all that other nonsense. We alternated between his house and mine, although we mostly ended up at my place on 16th Street.

Milo had a car, so we spent a lot of time outside of the city, too; weekends at the Eastern Shore, Rehoboth, Virginia Beach. We drove to his grandmother's house in West Virginia for our first 4th of July together. His grandmother was more open-minded than I would have expected for a woman of 88 and made us feel comfortable and loved. But these were only weekends. During the week we'd talk on the phone, see each other for dinner, return to one of our houses for a full-body massage and hours of mutual masturbation. One or the other would leave and we'd sleep alone during the week.

Now, not five hundred paces from my house was a man who whistled at me every time I passed his window. Two and a half weeks after his first whistle, I acknowledged him. His persistence won hands down over what I considered one of my greatest talents: an iron will and the tendency to be incredibly stubborn.

He had, at some point, established a pattern, a mating dance, if you will. As I approached the apartment building, I could see him, or at least the back of his head, in the window. He would be sitting on the couch, watching the news, or some reruns. Just as I got to the building entrance, he would look over his brawny and smooth shoulder, out the window. He would stand up, lean on the windowsill and watch me walk, as slowly and innocently as I could, to the corner. By then, he was standing in the bay window, a swag lamp glowing dimly behind him. Then, he would whistle.

August in Washington is like turning on the oven and leaving the door open. It's like having big kettles of boiling water, on all four burners of the stove, going at once. And then someone holds a magnifying glass between you and the sun. Someone once told me that diplomats and ambassadors used to get hardship pay for their stays in Washington in August. Clothing becomes an obstruction to comfort.

The whistler wore red running shorts or blue and white vertically striped running shorts or black running shorts, and nothing else. His shoulders looked wide enough to carry the world. His arms were muscular and defined; I could see the veins from my vantage point on the street corner. There was a chiseled separation between his pectorals. I wasn't sure, but I thought I detected a small patch of hair in the crevice. He seemed to be tan, and his nipples were as dark as Godiva chocolate. The window ledge began mid-thigh, where his shorts ended.

He was cute, too. Short, brown hair combed back. Big, blue eyes that always seemed to be on the verge of winking. And he smiled so much I wondered how he found time to whistle. I smiled back, finally. After all, there was no harm in smiling. I smiled and then a few days later, I nodded. He smiled, he nodded, he touched himself.

I closed up like one of those underwater flowers, like a Venus flytrap. Suddenly, the whistler-smiler-nodder wanted more than I could offer. Sinless flirtation coming dangerously close to the jagged, erotic line that could never be crossed. I had a lover. Who lived in Baltimore. That I saw on weekends. Well, most weekends.

He touched himself and I could make out the outline of something bigger than both of us. I crossed the street quicker than usual and didn't bother looking back, as I had begun to do. I just kept walking, both arms moving as if to propel me safely to my front gate. Watching my feet, the sidewalk. Trying not to be conscious of George Michael singing, "I Want Your Sex," blasting from my Walkman, the car parked across the street, the window of Jack's bedroom.

I called Milo that night. We talked about our plans for the weekend. He would drive down to Washington on Friday. My boss Gigi was going to cut his hair. On Saturday, while I was at work, he would help Bob and Jack paint and wallpaper the kitchen. We had tickets for a concert at Lisner Auditorium that night. We had dinner reservations at our favorite restaurant on M Street. He was going to spend the whole weekend, Sunday included. As we talked, I waited for him to tell me that something had come up, that he was going to have to cancel, again. I waited, anticipating every vowel. I realized I had drifted off, that I wasn't paying attention to what he was saying.

So, when he said that he'd see me at Bouffant Circle, at 4:00 on Friday, I had to ask him to repeat himself. He laughed, that hypnotic laugh of his, and said that he loved me more than frozen grapes and that he couldn't wait to see me and kiss me and taste me and sleep and sweat with me on Friday. And Saturday and Sunday, I added. And he agreed. And we hung up and I wondered how I would make it, on a Tuesday night, until Friday, without changing my route home or relocating altogether.

On Wednesday, I walked up F Street to 7th. I took the long way home. I couldn't help it. I couldn't risk losing control, now that things with Milo and me seemed to be back on track. This weekend would be a new beginning. Maybe I would leave Washington entirely. Start fresh in a new city with the man I loved. Everything looked brighter, as if I'd been viewing things through a dirty lint screen and now it was clean.

Wednesday night, I got a craving for a bowl of Life cereal. I went downstairs in my grey sweatpants and Silence=Death t-shirt. I got my favorite big bowl down from the cabinet above the microwave oven. I found a recently washed soup spoon in the strainer. I poured the cereal into the bowl until it was almost even with the lip. Then I discovered there was no milk in the refrigerator.

I left the bowl of dry cereal on the kitchen counter and ran upstairs. Sometimes at night it got cool, so I grabbed my Levi jacket and slipped my bare feet into a pair of old Nike running shoes. I knocked on Bob's door, but Jack called out from his room that he'd gone out for the night to a movie with some friends. I stood in the doorway of Jack's room, which was next to the bathroom, and asked him if he needed anything from the convenience store on Maryland Avenue. He was sitting up in bed, eating a bag of Utz crab-seasoned potato chips and watching a video of *The Way We Were*. He had a box of Kleenex on his lap. He smacked his lips and sniffled and said he was fine, thanked me for asking. I told him I'd be back in a few minutes.

It was an almost perfect summer night. People were sitting on their porches, on their stoops, talking and drinking and laughing. The air smelled like bar-b-q and flowers. Every car that drove by had its windows down and no two cars had the same song coming from their radios. Children darted in and out of each other's front yards, playing Freeze Tag or Statue. A constant breeze carried sounds and smells around the corner and out of reach. I crossed against the lights at Maryland and 8th.

Once inside the convenience store, I realized that I'd left my money at home. Luckily, I found my ATM card in my jacket pocket. I got in line behind two women who were arguing about what kind of beer to buy after they got their money. I recognized one of them as a waitress from Mr. Henry's on Pennsylvania Avenue, a restaurant Milo and I went to for Sunday brunch, when he still lived in the neighborhood.

When I got to the head of the line, I inserted my card and punched in my secret code. I took out twenty dollars which came out as two mutilated tens. I walked up and down the narrow aisles, looking at the shelves jammed full of overpriced food. Even though milk was the only thing I ever bought at this store, I always walked around as if I was going on a shopping spree. The stock was a constant, dusty and unchanged. I doubted that they ever rotated the merchandise.

At the counter I admired the displays of beef jerky and chewing gum especially for denture wearers. One of the clerks, in a logoed smock, was refilling the pornography rack behind the counter, occasionally flipping through one or two magazines that caught his interest.

The clerk at the cash register was voiding the purchases of the man in front of me, because the convenience store didn't accept travelers checks. The man kept saying, I thought these things were honored everywhere, I've never heard of such a thing, wait till I get back to Springfield. Missouri, Illinois, or Massachusetts, I wondered but decided against asking him.

Instead of walking down 8th Street to E Street, I decided to walk down Maryland to 6th Street. I wanted to walk past my friends' Daniel and Tom's house and see if they were home. There was a man walking two Dalmatians coming towards me. He had shoulder-length blonde hair and a few days growth of beard. He seemed to be younger than me from what I could tell by the streetlamps. He was very thin, but in a healthy way. As we got closer to each other, he opened his mouth to speak, but a car blew its horn as it drove past which made the dogs bark madly and he had to calm them down, untangle their leashes. I didn't look back, I kept on walking.

All the lights were off at Daniel and Tom's house. I'd left my watch at home, so I didn't know what time it was. I crossed Maryland where D Street cuts in and walked down D Street to 6th. Just a few blocks in from the busy street a sudden hush fell through the air. Even my footsteps sounded muffled, as if I was walking on the sidewalk in my bare feet. Air conditioners and fans pulsed in the windows of some of the houses. Others just had their windows thrown open all the way, screens between the outside and the inside.

Before I knew it, I was at the corner of 6th and E. Every light was on in the whistler's apartment. All the windows on E Street and 6th Street glowed like a landing strip, a beacon in a lighthouse. As I stood there, like an insect attracted to the heat of a candle, he came into the living room in a pair of white jockey shorts. He didn't stop and sit down on the couch; he didn't crouch to look out the window below the blinds. He walked straight to the bay window on the corner and looked out. If my mouth weren't so dry, I would have whistled.

He put his hands on his hips. I imagined he was tapping his foot slowly, patiently, beating out a rhythm that matched my heartbeat. The Don't Walk sign blinked in syncopation. There wasn't a moving car in sight. I crossed the street on a diagonal. From the sidewalk, there was some grass and some glass between us.

Come on up, he said and walked back into the living room. I stayed where I was. No, I said. Yes, he said, come inside, and he kneeled on the couch and raised the mini blind a hair. He opened the window a little wider. I watched the muscles in his arms move.

I have to go home, I said. No, you don't, he said and stood up and walked out of the living room. My heart seemed to stop. I couldn't see him. Where had he gone? And then I heard him say, I'll buzz you in. I looked up at the small kitchen window to the right of the apartment building entrance. What if I don't want to come in? I said. I don't want to come in. Oh yes, you do, he said, and I want you to come in. I clutched the half-gallon carton of 2% milk to my chest. It felt cool through the jacket and t-shirt.

I have to put the milk in the refrigerator, I said. I have a refrigerator, he said, come on, come in.

The security door buzzed loudly and I was afraid the neighbors would run to their windows if I didn't go to the door and open it, so he would stop pressing the button. I opened the door, walked up five steps. The buzzing echoed in my head, rang like an unanswered phone. He was waiting for me in the doorway of his apartment.

When I stand straight, I'm probably five foot nine and one half, although my driver's license says five foot ten. Milo and I see eye to eye although I may be a fraction taller. The whistler was at least six foot one. I leaned my head back a little to meet his eyes and he pressed his open mouth on mine. He had a tongue with a mind of its own that moved slowly across all my teeth and then probed almost to the back of my throat. He wrapped his arms around me so tightly, I was afraid he'd crush the milk carton, so I pushed him away, our mouths still attached.

We bent slightly, together, so I could put the bag on the floor. On the way back up he removed my jacket in one swift tug and began to lift my t-shirt over my head. Since we were joined at the mouth, I was certain that he was going to rip the t-shirt off. Just as suddenly as he'd started, he stopped kissing me. Take it off, he said, now. The t-shirt was off me and on the floor in record time. He pulled me to him and the hairs on our chests met. He half-carried, half-swept me into his bedroom at the end of a short corridor which also led to the kitchen, living room and bathroom.

I fell on top of him on the king-size bed. He managed to work the jockey shorts off and his huge, hard cock throbbed between us. He struggled with a knot in my sweatpants while licking my chin, my Adam's apple and the rest of my neck. The string was untied, and he slipped his hand into the sweatpants and gripped my hard-on. With the other hand he tugged on one of my nipples. Ouch, I said, not really meaning it and he let go. He wrapped his legs around mine. He held both of our cocks in one hand, each curving up and away from the other and moved the skin back and forth. We were kissing again, our tongues slopping around inside each other's mouths. Both of our eyes wide open and staring wildly into the others. His eyes were not as blue as Milo's.

Suddenly, I closed my mouth around both of our tongues. I gently spit his tongue back into his mouth. I put my hands on his immense shoulders and pushed myself up, off the bed, into a standing position. My stiff dick was pointing at him like an indicator. What's wrong, he asked, the look on his face a combination of arousal and confusion. I have to go, I said. Go, he repeated, go where? You just got here. I have to go home, I said. Please don't go, he said. I'll put the milk in the refrigerator if you're worried about it, he said, just don't go.

I have to go, I said, and began to pull the sweatpants up from around my ankles. He sat up, resting on his elbows. He watched me stuff my still erect cock into the sweatpants. It was pointing at him. I felt like a compass. He was a porno magazine dreamboy come to life. It was obvious, looking at him, that he'd worked out long and hard for that body. I tied the string and adjusted myself. He sat up quickly and untied it; pressed his face into my crotch. He brought his arms up behind me, around me. No, I said, please. And he let go.

Why are you leaving, he asked, what's wrong with me? Nothing, I said, I just have to go. Can't you at least tell me why? he asked. I looked at him. I was in his apartment, in his bedroom. I wanted to stay. I have a lover, I said. A lover, he repeated. Yes, I said. Where is he, he asked, where is your lover? In Baltimore, I said. In Baltimore, he said like the world's sexiest echo. Yes, I said, in Baltimore. I have to go.

If your lover is in Baltimore, he asked, what are you doing here? I wasn't sure if he meant here in his apartment or here in Washington. What do you mean? I asked. Why aren't you with him, he asked, doesn't he know how lucky he is to have you? Isn't he afraid that someone might come along and steal you away? Someone like me? He believes in me, I said, in us. And you, he said, do you believe? Yes, I said, I believe.

As I walked around the bed to the door of the bedroom, he fell back on the bed, his head hanging over the end so he could see upside down, out the door, down the short corridor to where I stood, putting on my t-shirt. I meant what I said, he said, about your lover being lucky. I know, I said, I meant what I said, too. I put my jacket on and he got out of bed walked toward me with his cock still semi-erect. His cock was as beautiful as the rest of him. I wanted you to fuck me, he said, I wanted to feel you all the way inside me. He held my face in his hands and kissed me in a way that made me instantly hard again.

We bent slightly so that I could pick up the brown paper bag with the carton of milk in it. Let me know if it doesn't work out, he said. You know where to find me, I said. All you have to do is whistle, I said. You know how to whistle, don't you?

CHOCOLATE DIPPED

It's funny, don't you think, the way an accident can become a habit. Unclear, though, how a habit develops into a ritual. Then, before you know it, the ritual transforms itself into a fetish. Shoplifters, for instance, are said to get a sexual charge from quickly, discreetly slipping something unpaid for into their coat pockets or purses, boldly strutting toward the exit. But is it the thrill of the act or the threat of getting caught that can repeatedly bring the petty criminal to the brink of orgasm? Ask a fire starter or the person who follows the sound of sirens to the scene of the head-on collision in a busy intersection, if they know what it is about these events that make the tops of their heads feel as if they might become unattached.

My lover Cary and I were cleaning up our apartment after my sister, brother-in-law, and two nephews Cruise and Willis, went home. They were the last of the stragglers from my biological family, that had attended our annual friends-and-family winter-holiday party. At a little after midnight, Cary and I were both on the receiving end of what amounted to a second wind. We both enjoyed entertaining, did it frequently and, weren't averse to leaving dirty glasses and dishes in the kitchen sink if we could see the sun coming up over Lake Michigan, through the kitchen window, which wasn't an unusual occurrence after any one of our parties throughout the calendar year. However, the combination of the cold temperature outside, the threat of a potential Chicago snowstorm, and the presence of family members of all ages, guaranteed that this party would not be one of those.

Cary was the one who had suggested that we invite our respective families to what had traditionally been a party consisting of our chosen family. Over the years, four to be exact, our "chosen" family began to include members of Cary's biological family. Initially, it had been Cary's first cousin Jon who cracked the barrier of the family, and that was only because he came out to us at Cary's parents' 40th wedding anniversary party, and we soon began to socialize on a regular basis.

At first, I was a little jealous. I didn't have any gay cousins. As far as I knew, I didn't have any gay relatives at all. From all appearances, I was the one exception to the heterosexual rule in my clan, but, fortunately for me, I was never ostracized or treated any differently by any of my immediate family members after I came out at the age of twenty-two.

Eventually, our "all-inclusive" holiday party (Christmas, Solstice, Kwanza, Hanukkah, and any other winter holiday of note) also grew to include our blood relatives. In surveying the damage from the evening's entertainment, it appeared we had emerged unscathed. In fact, we felt quite proud of our achievement. We threw a party consisting of some forty (including significant others) invited guests, and tossed our relatively small families (my parents, sister, brother-in-law, and nephews, Cary's recently-widowed father, his two older brothers, and their wives) into the mix, and nothing was spilled that couldn't be cleaned up, or broken that couldn't be fixed or discarded without too much fuss.

I'm not sure what it was then, that possessed us to do the clean-up in the buff. Perhaps one or the other of us had become aware of the smoky smell that permeated our holiday finery, even though all our smoking guests had been instructed to do so on the balcony. It was such a blustery night that the cigarette smoke managed to be blown into the room every time a smoker returned from the outside, opening and trying their best to close the balcony door as quickly as possible. Maybe it was just that it was very warm in the apartment. The heat had been on all night, and it was as if the walls of the apartment, the furniture and the area rugs, had managed to retain some of our guests' body heat.

Whatever it was, we were suddenly, scurrying about, collecting wine glasses and empty beer bottles, festive paper coffee cups and crumpled napkins, messy paper plates and plastic silverware, and filling the tall, black Hefty kitchen garbage bags, naked as the day we were born. There was already a garbage bag filled to the brim with glittery wrapping paper scraps from the grab-bag gift exchange. It was tied up tight, looking like something mummified, and leaning against a wall in the kitchen.

"There's something sticky on this table," Cary said, kneeling on his bare, lightly hairy knees, before the vintage teak coffee table in front of the oversized sofa, running his fingers over something blurring the surface.

"Do you want a moist sponge or a paper towel?" I asked, heading for the kitchen, while keeping my ear cocked for his response.

"Paper towel, I think," he said, "and a couple of dry ones, too, please."

I grabbed a half-full garbage bag and collected trash on my way into the kitchen situated at the other end of the apartment. I wasn't watching where I was going and, five steps into the kitchen I stepped on something gooey and slick, feeling it adhere to the bottom of my bare foot while it ground into a couple of the black and white checkerboard parquet squares beneath me. I righted myself before twisting my back too much, and simply said, "Shit!"

"Noah? Did you say something?" Cary called out from his watchful station in front of the sticky stain on the table.

"I said, 'Shit,'" I said, looking down to determine what it was that I had stepped in and smeared across the floor. A few inches away from where I was standing were the empty bent gold foil discs that I recognized as the covering for the large milk chocolate "coin" I had stepped on. Who knew how long it had been sitting there, out of its protective wrapping? Apparently long enough to have softened up to a mushy, not crumbly, consistency.

Earlier in the evening, when Cary gave my nephews their little plastic mesh bags of chocolate Hanukkah "gelt," he had specifically told them that when they wanted to eat one, that the kitchen was the place to do so. If there was one thing I could say for my older sister Ina, and her husband Jim, it was that her children always did as they were told. Just as I was about to try to decipher whether it was Cruise or Willis who had done this, Cary came into the room.

"Is that your imitation of a pink flamingo?" Cary asked over my shoulder.

When he said that, I realized that I had been standing on one leg, with my right, chocolate-smudged foot crossed over my left knee.

"I stepped in something," I said, pointing to the darkened soul of my bare foot. Cary moved closer to me, his soft body hair brushing against my bare back. He stood a full head taller than me, and as I leaned back against him, I felt the crown of my head make contact with his Adam's apple.

Earlier in the evening, at the party, I became aware that I was not making as much physical contact with Cary as I usually did in social situations. We've earned a reputation among those who know us for being something of a demonstrative couple, completely at ease with ourselves and our relationship. While we never do it to shock anyone, we are, within reason, prone to public displays of affection. But for some unknown reason, the presence of both of our families, perhaps, I felt myself holding back. At one point during the party, Cary became especially animated, while telling a particularly funny story. I felt this sudden urge to excuse both of us from our guests, while we took to our bedroom, to alleviate the unexpected hard-on I felt expanding within my khakis.

He nuzzled the back of my neck, and before I had a chance to put my chocolate-coated foot on the floor, he wrapped his arms around my waist, lifted me up, and carried me to the kitchen counter near the sink. He helped me ease my bare butt onto the cool, and slightly cluttered Corian surface. For a second, I was embarrassed by our nakedness in the kitchen, but one look at his completely erect penis told me I had nothing to worry about.

I waited for him to turn on the tap so that we could rinse off my foot and was surprised when he crouched down in front of me. He took my chocolate splattered foot in both hands and proceeded to lick the sweetness off my skin. I felt his tongue on my heel, then his lips, and just a tease of teeth. It tickled in a different way than fingers did. It felt like fingers wrapped in warm velvet. He dropped one of his hands between his legs and alternately pulled on and stroked his erection, as his tongue and lips moved sweetly across the arch of my foot. He turned my foot sideways, stretching his mouth open wider, gripping it gently with his teeth, while he ran his tongue back and forth across the most tender part of the flesh.

I had been using my hands to support myself on the counter-top, which had warmed up enough for me to move one hand into my lap and over my boner. I reached over to the bottle of environmentally safe dish-washing liquid to lube myself with, when Cary tightened his grip on my foot. Our eyes met and with only the slightest motion, he shook his head no, his chocolate-coated lips and tongue making their way to the ball of my foot and my toes.

"Kiss me on the mouth," I said, "I want something sweet, too."

Cary stood up, his erection not allowing him to get too close to the kitchen cabinets and looked at me smiling. He had the look of a little boy who had just stolen all of the just-baked, still warm, chocolate chip cookies off the rack where they had been cooling and eaten every last one. My first urge was to find something with which to wipe off his mouth and chin, the tip of his nose. Instead, I wrapped my legs around his waist, my arms around his neck and kissed long and hard.

While we were kissing, he reached up to the cabinets behind me, where we kept the spices and the baking supplies, and pulled out an unopened bag of Nestlé's Tollhouse chocolate chips. He opened the cabinet below where I was sitting and retrieved a pot. He pulled away from me and tore into the bag of chocolate chips, pouring more than half the bag into the pot and putting it on the stove, a low, blue flame pulsing from the burner. He came back to where I was sitting, looking at him with eyes both dejected and curious. He kissed me quickly, jamming his still chocolaty tongue between my lips, as he retrieved a wooden spoon from the drawer below where I was sitting.

At the stove, he stirred the pot with his back to me. His shoulders were wide from years of regular workouts at the gym. His back was modestly muscular and hairless, narrowing down to his hips, and his slightly furry bubble-butt. His legs were nicely defined and slightly bowed, the hair from his butt-cheeks growing darker and a little thicker on his thighs and calves, stopping where his ankles met his feet. I wanted to go to him, my erection losing a little of its hardness. I tried to move discreetly off the counter-top, but my hairless buttocks made a squeaky sound when I moved forward.

"Stay where you are," Cary said, "I'll be right there. All the chips have almost melted."

In less than a minute, what he said was true, and I watched him pour the liquefied chocolate chips, which let off a whisper of steam as it flowed, dark and slow as proverbial molasses, into a soup bowl. Using his foot, he dragged the step stool I used to reach things on the upper shelves of the kitchen cabinets, over to where he had been standing in front of me and stepped up, giving himself, and his unflagging erection some leverage, and allowing me an unobstructed view of more of him. Without speaking, he spread my legs apart, making room on the counter for the bowl of hot chocolate. He cupped my genitals in both hands, scooping them up, while slightly tipping the bowl back toward my groin. He released me and there was a thick, slow-motion splashing sound.

When my cock and balls made contact with the chocolate dip, it felt as warm as a mouth. My dick quickly regained its hardness, skimming the bottom of the bowl, then rising out of it, like a water-borne creature surfacing from the deep. The tips of my pubic hair, closest to the base of my dick, were frosted in chocolate, glistening briefly, before drying and clumping together. He massaged the chocolate into the taut skin of my dick and balls, it felt so good, I sighed, as if close to orgasm.

"Don't you dare," he said, recognizing the familiar sound.

"I won't," I said.

He crouched down, again, still on the step stool, both feet dangling off the edge of the narrow surface, and began to lick and suck my chocolate-dipped dick. His lips smacked with every motion he made, forward and back. He sucked each chocolaty ball gently into his mouth, grazing them with his teeth. And when they emerged from between his lips, the skin was only lightly veined with chocolate.

"Lay back," he said, his voice thick with chocolate, and I did.

Some of the chocolate must have streaked down below my balls, into the space above my asshole, because his tongue followed a trail down there, slurping, as he went. His chocolate-stained thumbs spread my ass-cheeks and I figured that Cary either found more chocolate spillage or that he wanted to personally introduce my prostate to chocolate with his tongue. Even without touching myself, I knew I was dangerously close to coming with Cary's mouth firmly planted between my buttocks and his chocolate-breath melting my defenses.

"Cary, if you don't stop that, I won't be able to hold back much longer."

He stood up and leaned over me, planting a kiss on my mouth that tasted like a mocha version of me. Our lips detached, and he was back at the stove. There was a little chocolate in the bottom of the pot that only took a few seconds to heat up and turn into a sexy cocoa-based sauce, sufficient to coat the head of Cary's still rock-hard cock. He smoothed it into the head, working as methodically as a safecracker. He scooped the remaining chocolate from the pot with the index and middle fingers of his other hand. He subtly moved his head from side to side, indicating to me that he wanted my ankles on his shoulders.

I eased the lower half of my body forward, while leaning back, careful not to knock anything over. It was a surprisingly graceful move in a limited space. As soon as my heels made contact with his shoulders, his chocolate-slicked fingers were sliding gently in and out of my asshole. I had never before considered the lubricating qualities of chocolate and was surprised by the silky texture. Just as I was beginning to enjoy the sensation of his fingers, I felt something more substantial in their place.

My eyes went wide and my head was thrown back like a Pez dispenser. He was halfway in before I let out a sweetened grunt. Such an action was completely out of character for both of us, advocates of safe sex and long lives, but we were obviously under the spell of the chocolate narcotic. Still, we both knew that the chocolate would have probably done more damage than good to a condom, and experience had taught us not to do anything foolish.

I grabbed my fudgesicle dick and stroked it in rhythm to Cary's thrusts. He pulled out after a few minutes, our orgasms synchronized, our cum like white chocolate pools on my chest and stomach, only sweetened the deal.

While I never considered either of us creatures of habit, before long, anything chocolate or chocolate-coated was stockpiled for variations on this theme. Once, after shaving Cary's chest and armpits, I slathered his upper torso in Frango mint chocolate, and spent more than an hour licking him clean. We tried Belgian chocolate and Hershey's syrup. We pelted our fannies in Fannie May and Fannie Farmer. We'll never look at a Whitman Sampler in quite the same way again. You can only imagine what happened to the five-pound, red-satin, chocolate-filled, heart-shaped boxes of candy we exchanged on Valentine's Day, can't you?

I'm just thankful I didn't step in peanut butter or raw liver.

THE SHORT STORY OF MY LIFE

1.

Soon after my ex-boyfriend Paul was ordained as a Catholic priest, he informed me that nothing had changed between us. How soon, you ask? Mere minutes.

Of course, you haven't lived until you've watched someone with whom you've done unspeakable acts lying prostrate on the altar before God. It's like attending the wedding of a former flame; but your former flame is marrying Jesus.

Fortunately, my good friends Joey and Theo and Brian were there with me at the ordination to prevent me from doing something I'd regret. They were literally holding me down in the pew. Theo to my left and Brian to my right had a tight grip on my elbows and forearms, while Joey, from behind, put the most loving amount of pressure he could put on my neck and shoulders without causing me to lose consciousness. What did they think I was going to do? Pull a Dustin Hoffman in *The Graduate*?

What was I thinking? What sane person would attend such an event? What I was thinking is that I didn't really need much of an excuse to fly from Chicago to Philadelphia to get away from the domestic disturbance that was my presently disintegrating relationship with Jesse.

Here's where it gets sketchy. Before Paul and I became an item, Jesse and I had been together for a few years. After Jesse and I officially broke up (the first time) and I met Paul, I was ready to settle into a relationship with more affection and fewer afflictions.

During my relationship with Paul, some unforeseen things occurred. For instance, the family dog, Nyro, was reaching the end of her life. Just how close she was to the end of her life I observed firsthand upon returning to my parents' house in Milwaukee at Christmas.

The unidentifiable and immobile shape in the corner of the dining room was not my mother's latest abandoned crochet project, but, in fact, ancient Nyro. My parents had conveniently skipped town with my younger brother, leaving me and my older brother in charge of Nyro's end-of-life strategy. Being the kind and loving brothers we are (if not to each other, then at least to Nyro), we immediately scheduled an appointment for her to be euthanized.

In seriously bad emotional shape following such an unexpected and tragic event, I was unprepared for a phone call from Jesse who also happened to be back in Milwaukee visiting his family for the holiday. At this point, Jesse and I had already been broken up for more than two years. Which is why his phone call was such a surprise, and not in a good way.

Always a master of timing (if not fidelity), Jesse heard the distress in my voice and offered to come over and comfort me. In other words, he knew I was vulnerable and saw it as a perfect chance for him to take advantage of my weakened state, which is exactly what he did. Seizing the opportunity, Jesse begged me to come back to Chicago with him and give our relationship another chance. I caved.

In the meantime, Paul, an ex-seminarian when I met him, decided to "return to school," as he put it. Unrepentant heathen that I am, I didn't realize that "school" was another word for seminary. He assured me that our relationship was of the utmost importance to him. But his low-paying social worker job felt like a dead-end and he wanted to make something of himself. I, on the other hand, enjoyed my job in the front office of a weekly gay newspaper in DuPont Circle, where I answered phones, greeted visitors, handled the classified ads and occasionally wrote movie reviews.

Returning to school meant that Paul would have to leave Washington, DC, where we cohabitated, and head north to Philadelphia. He even lined up a roommate to share the living expenses on our Adams Morgan flat. That's the kind of thoughtful guy Paul is. He just wasn't thoughtful enough to mention that he was returning to school to become, you know, a priest.

Meanwhile, back at the OK cathedral, I was looking for a wall to scale, a tower to commandeer and a bell to ring; something to silence all the nagging questions in my head. Once the coast was clear, and the handful of new priests left the altar for wherever it is that newly ordained priests go, Theo, Brian and Joey loosened their combined hold on me. Certain that I wasn't going to leap across the pews and make a scene, they set about massaging their hands and fingers, waiting for the feeling to return after applying such a tight grip.

We all smiled sad smiles at each other. They felt my pain. Doing everything I could to contain what I feared would be foaming at the mouth; I excused myself and headed to the men's room. I wanted to freshen up before the luncheon on the cathedral grounds, sponsored by Paul's newly divorced parents.

Let me tell you, there's no better place to lose it than in the men's room of a cathedral. The echo factor alone makes it all worthwhile. I sobbed, I raged, I laughed, I babbled, I sniffled and snorted. After pulling myself together and making my exit, I discovered that several men were waiting on line outside of the women's restroom, considerate and thoughtful enough not to disturb me in my time of need and unbalance.

An expert at avoidance, I found an unexplored cathedral corridor and immediately headed in that direction. Stone walls and benches lined one side of the long hallway, while a stained-glass tableau ran opposite, letting in enough colorful light to allow my teary eyes time to adjust before lunch was served.

As I got about a quarter of the way down the length of the passageway, Paul rounded the corner from the other direction. He was looking down at his feet as he walked, adjusting his priest's collar with his index finger. As soon as he saw me, a smile more radiant than the sun beaming through the stained glass spread across his face. I stopped dead in my tracks. I couldn't move. If I did, I was convinced that I would turn to cinders and that Paul would use my remains to draw crosses on people's foreheads on Ash Wednesday.

I didn't have to move. Paul came to me. He embraced me, right there in his boss' house, our instant erections creating a modified cross, as they met through our pants. How can this not be wrong? I thought in my own ill-informed way. But dark storm clouds didn't appear to block the radiance of the sun illuminating us in this hall. No lightning struck us down. No angels appeared to point us down a different hotter and darker path, no demons snickered with approval.

Paul hugged me and I returned his hold, wondering what would happen to my spine once he let go. Would I go slack or stand straighter and taller than ever? I kept my eyes open the whole time, watchful of anyone approaching us.

With his lips as near to my ear as they could get without actually being inside, Paul said, "Nothing has changed. Nothing."

It was then that I closed my eyes.

2.

A man of his word, as well as a man of God, Paul arranged a series of rendezvous for us beginning a few short weeks after his ordination. It was not uncommon for me to travel as part of my job as the entertainment editor at a gay lifestyle magazine in Chicago, a gig I was able to line up after leaving DC. Press junkets abounded, although most of them took me to L.A. or New York.

Jesse was used to my schedule and, in his own way, enjoyed it. With me out of sight, he could trick freely. That's right. Jesse, who broke up my first relationship with Paul to rekindle our own questionably stable one, had a serious problem with fidelity. A serial monogamist myself, I decided to look the other way as a long as Jesse played safe and was regularly tested for HIV and the gamut of STIs.

By this point, however, my attitude was beginning to change. Why was I wasting my time, again, in a relationship with Jesse when we clearly wanted different things? I wanted a lover and he wanted lovers. With that in mind, I didn't see the harm in having my own dalliance.

Without even making up an excuse, I made frequent trips to DC. To our delight, Theo and Brian were not only unsurprised at the way Paul and I resumed our relationship, they were supportive and encouraging. Not big fans of Jesse, Theo and Brian offered us a room in their spacious home for our conjugal visits. When they were unable to accommodate us, we'd check into a hotel, say the Holiday Inn near Thomas Circle, order each other around and then order room service.

Before long, we were talking about making our tenuous situation a more permanent one. How, I wondered? Would I take up residence in the rectory in Old City? Were there other priests who had similar arrangements? Was

God too busy starting wars and designing diseases to pay attention to a priest with an age-appropriate boyfriend?

I was also concerned about how out we could be as a couple. As someone who came out to his family at 17, I couldn't imagine going back into the closet at 31. Paul assured me that it wouldn't be an issue, that we would find a way to make it work. That he would fight to change the system from within. While he was at it, I wondered if he could also find the time to cure AIDS and cancer, to end world hunger and create everlasting global peace.

3.

Then this happened. Alice, an old friend from college, won a big literary prize and moved from Chicago's Andersonville neighborhood to Washington DC. That's right. After years of teaching creative writing at a community college in a Chicago suburb and consistently publishing her humorously violent poetry in a variety of journals and magazines, Alice shoots and scores. She is wooed away to the prestigious Washington, DC University, where she will teach a total of two poetry workshops and make four times the salary she was earning at Skokie Community College.

Alice and her girlfriend Gert (I kid you not) were aware of the situation with Paul, whom they called Father Daddy. As lapsed Catholics frustrated by the Church's treatment of the gay community, they were all for any subversive activity, the gayer the better.

"If you move to Philadelphia to be with Paul, you'll be much closer to us in DC than if you stay here in Chicago with the Prince of Promiscuity," Alice said.

We were in the Foster Avenue condo she shared with Gert, packing boxes of books for their impending move. Alice had a point. There was a reason they called Philadelphia "the city of brotherly love." I felt loved by it and the idea of starting a life there with Paul. My boyfriend, the priest. And I preferred eating crabs with Paul to getting them from Jesse.

Then I got cold feet. There were too many variables. I didn't want to risk Paul losing everything he had worked so hard for if, for some reason, our relationship caused a problem within his parish or with the higher-ups; including the Most High. Following one of the rare visits he made to see me in Chicago, where we blew our wad, so to speak, on a weekend at The Drake, I called it quits. Believe me, no one was more stunned than I was.

4.

This is where things really get weird.

To call my break-up with Paul amicable would be an understatement. He knew my concerns and had sensed my hesitation for some time, and he took it well; better than I did. After all we'd been through this strengthened our love for each other, ensuring that we would have a close friendship unlike any others we'd ever had.

Enter Matt. A former neighbor of Theo and Brian's whom I had met a few times when they were still Cleveland Park apartment dwellers. Matt had lived in the unit next door with his then-boyfriend Ken. Theo and Matt both worked on Capitol Hill for senators on opposite sides of the aisle. Somehow gay men on the Hill were able to overlook issues such as the relentless Republican attack on all things gay in the name of friendship (and whatever else might arise).

Together for four years, Matt and Ken broke up not long after their fourth anniversary and Ken moved out of the apartment. Theo and Brian offered Matt a shoulder to cry on and a place in their social circle. That social circle, as it turns out, also included Paul, whom they got to know when he and I were a couple.

By this time, I had recommitted to Jesse and relocated from DC to Chicago. I kept in touch with Paul on a regular basis. He updated me on his life as a parish priest. It was as fulfilling as he'd imagined. It kept him so busy he hardly had time to think about how alone he felt without me. Mentioning it to me seemed to be proof of that. Still, Paul managed to carve out time for a social life, which included attending a 40th birthday party for Brian. Among the other guests on the list was, you guessed it, Matt.

As luck would have it, Matt saw something in Paul and vice versa. Before you can sing "Love Is In the Air," Paul and Matt became a hot and heavy item. I found out on New Year's Eve, when Paul called to wish me a happy new one and share the news. I have to admit to having mixed emotions.

I was, as it turns out, still in love with Paul, a fact that became increasingly clear as I realized what a mistake I had made getting back together with Jesse. Despite promising to have changed his wandering ways, Jesse was one leopard who had trouble maintaining his spots. For a moment, the future looked like this: another break-up with Jesse on the horizon, while Paul, who I'm reminding you took a vow of celibacy, was about to break that vow with someone who wasn't me. It was too much for me to bear.

Now, here's an edited version of a Washington DC to Chicago phone call between me and Alice -

Alice: How's my little Blueberry Muffin doing?

Me: Bluer than blue.

Alice: Sounds like you need some muff love. Why's that?

Me: Looks like me and Jesse are through, again.

Alice: Praise the goddess!

Me: Uh, really? That's the best you can do? How about a little compassion?

Alice: Compassion shmassion. I saw this coming from here and so did you.

Me: Maybe, maybe not. But still…

Alice: Listen, kiddo, since you already have an open wound, please excuse me while I pour some salt in it.

Me: Do I need to sit down or lie down?

Alice: You might want to stay away from any open flames. You'll never guess who Gert and I crossed paths with while getting off the elevator in the lobby of our building yesterday.

Me: Hillary Clinton.

Alice: So close, yet so far. Paul.

Me: Paul, as in my Paul?

Alice: He's not your Paul anymore, Muffin Man.

Me: Who's Paul is he?

Alice: He's Matt's Paul now, remember?

Me: How could I forget?

Alice: But wait, there's more.

Me: There's always room for more.

Alice: Aren't you going to ask me why Paul was getting on the elevator? Don't ask, I'll tell you. Paul was getting on the elevator because…

Me: …he doesn't like stairs.

Alice: Why I ought to…Paul was getting on the elevator to visit Matt. Matt lives in our building. Matt doesn't just live in our building; he lives on our floor. Matt doesn't just live in our building, on our floor, he lives across the hall.

And scene.

5.

You don't know this about me, but I'm the kind of person who gives nicknames to others. For example, Jesse is Messy. Yes, he is. Depending on her mood, Alice is Princess Poetry or Polly Pentameter (good), which could be shortened to PP, or A Lice or Malice (bad). Paul was My All (but I never shared that with anyone). Matt became Mattress.

The gorgeous art deco apartment building on Calvert Street, where Alice and Gert lived, with Mattress just across the hall, became a proverbial thorn in my side. I lived in fear of visiting them, which in turn would lead to potential Paul and Mattress sightings. I wasn't opposed to the idea of Paul being in a relationship. I just didn't want to have to see it. Of course, there was a double standard in play. Because shortly after Alice shared her news with me, I rang her up with news of my own.

Me: PP, I've met someone.

Alice: Spill, Muffin, spill.

Me: His name is Robby. He's the new editor-in-chief at *Look Out Magazine*. It was love at first sight.

Alice: I can't wait to tell Gert. I'm so happy for you, Muffin Man. You must bring him to your nation's capital so that we may poke and prod him, approve or disapprove.

That's how we ended up on this flight tonight; me and Robby, heading to DC to cover the latest exhibition of the Names Project AIDS Memorial Quilt. Alice and Gert insisted on playing host, even though we had offers to be put up in the five-star hotels of our choice, as well as at Theo and Brian's. Joey was also flying in from Philly to see the Quilt and was staying with his ex-boyfriend Tom. Talk about pressure, Robby wasn't just meeting Alice and Gert, he was going to be paraded before other forever friends of mine, all of whom, I was certain, would feel about him the way that I did.

On the cab ride from Washington National Airport to Alice and Gert's, Robby was going over the weekend's itinerary. I was half-listening, going over my own agenda of possible (or impossible) scenarios involving what would happen if I (or we) should find ourselves in the same elevator, Metro car or station, restaurant or bar, throng or huddled mass, as Paul and Mattress. My list included swooning, fainting, vomiting, crying, laughing, choking, choking Mattress, hysterical blindness, hysterical pregnancy, general hysteria, tinnitus, pleading the fifth, pleading insanity, hostility, hospitality, being crass and, ultimately, being goodness and kindness, love and light incarnate.

Regardless of the worry and fuss, the weekend took a decidedly different turn than anyone anticipated. Because a priest's work is never done, on call, like a doctor, Paul was forced to stay behind in Philadelphia to tend to a series of spiritual crises. He even called me on my mobile a few times during the weekend to apologize for not being able to see me, to meet Robby, to make a formal renewed introduction to Mattress, and to experience this final large public display of the Quilt on the Mall with all of us, and to offer comfort, if need be. What a man (of God)!

Suddenly, the threat of awkward social interaction didn't seem as threatening. That is until we were extended a series of invitations to gatherings before and after the planned candlelight vigil and march on the Capitol. One such gathering, would in fact, be taking place in Alice and Gert's apartment. Let me assure you, I was, to my own surprise, on my best behavior. Maybe I felt less threatened, standing securely with my man (and a handsome and muscled, nattily dressed one, at that) on my arm, when I came face-to-face with Mattress. Maybe Mattress was more charming and cuddly than I remembered him being when we first met years before.

He was a hugger, a cheek kisser. He thought nothing of slipping an arm over your shoulder or lacing his fingers through yours when he found himself next to you in a group or one-on-one conversation. Bordering on becoming a personal groomer, he casually brushed a stray hair out of my eye, gently plucked an eyelash from my cheek and insisted I make a wish and blow if off his fingertip. He did, however, control himself from wiping the sleep from my eyes. He straightened collars on shirts, smoothed creases on khakis. He patted my ass; not in a sexual way, but as friendly as all get out.

And so, even though I wasn't a priest, but in fact a dyed-in-the-womb atheist, I gave him and Paul what amounted to my blessing. Yes, I did. I finally let go and it felt good, like flying through the air on a swing in a playground. Like meeting someone you knew would be in your life for the rest of it; a lover and then husband, like Robby. A pal and a confidant, like Matt.

WIDE AWAKE ON HALSTED STREET

He bought me a bottled water at Manhole. I drank it down and drank him in, through hazy cigarette smoke and house music. He's half a head shorter than me, and I am fascinated with the part in his thick, dark hair. Even and straight, like a tightrope. I imagine my fingers walking in a line across his scalp.

He is undoing my belt buckle, strictly a backroom maneuver, out of place at the front bar. I pull away. It takes more than an Evian in a glass bottle to earn a gesture like that.

I live on Cornelia, he says.

Was that an invitation? I ask.

Are you accepting? he asks.

What will we do when we get there? I ask.

I'm stalling, because the last man I went home with from a bar became a two-year relationship that ended with all the finesse of a migraine headache. That won't happen tonight. Tonight, I'm going to fuck and run.

Let's talk about it on the walk to my place, he says. It'll distract us from thinking about how cold it is outside.

The doorman stamps the back of our hands, expecting one of us to return later. He takes my friend's drink from him as he tries to leave with it. He says, See you later, Steve.

We turn the corner and he shoves me against the brick wall, pins my shoulders back and affixes his mouth to mine. He tastes drunk. I am reminded of the cold.

I'm cold, I say without a trace of whine.

Let me warm you up, Steve says, dropping to his knees.

I bet it's warmer in your bed, I say.

When he stands up, I'd swear he's grown a few inches. He flings a solid, muscular arm around my shoulder. I slip a hand into the back waistband of his Levis, discover that he's not wearing any underwear. His ass is smooth and warm.

I stand close to him in the vestibule. He grinds his ass into my crotch while unlocking his apartment door. We are greeted by a Siamese cat that alternately berates me and brushes up against my ankles with the force of a Rottweiler.

Steve kicks off his hiking boots, drops his black leather jacket on the floor, pulls his button-down shirt over his head, all the while walking away from me. When he gets to his bedroom door, he turns to face me. His fat cock is pushing against the buttons of his 501s.

In his bedroom he undresses me slowly, like a lover. In his bed, we run the gamut of positions. He grips the headboard like handlebars while he rides my face. He is still wearing his white socks which seem to glow fluorescent on his black sheets. He pulls his dick out of my mouth, dragging it down my chin, Adam's apple and chest.

He puts his muscles to use, flipping me over on my stomach, pulling me to my knees, lifting my furry ass to his mouth. Although I am enjoying this, I can't see him. I want to look him in the eyes. The next day, when I tell my friend Bob about this, he will want to know the color of Steve's eyes.

I am not as strong as he is, but I find a way to flip myself over and wrap my legs around his narrow waist. We kiss again, tasting each other, and I turn him over. His ankles rest comfortably on my shoulders and he unwraps a condom, using both hands to fit me.

We stay still for a long time after I penetrate him. His grip is impressive. His eyes are brown. I move slowly and then speed up. Slow and fast. Slow, and then he comes without even touching himself, hitting his chin and both nipples, leaving a string of wet whiteness dissecting his flat belly. I fill the condom inside him.

We spoon and fondle for a little while, but I don't want to overstay my welcome. I don't want him to ask me to stay. I dress while he is in the bathroom, peeing with the door open. He walks me to the door like a gentleman.

I head back to Halsted Street at 3:45 a.m. to find a ride home. I don't hail just any cab; I wait for one of those new ones that looks like a whale on wheels. The flags flap. My teeth chatter. I still taste him on my lips and gums. He is drying on my skin, under my clothes. My hands are semen casts of themselves.

I want to start a conversation with the cab driver, certain he's caught a whiff of me leaving something behind on his new upholstery. Instead, I watch his peach-scented, pine-tree shaped air freshener dangle and twirl from the rear-view mirror. I contemplate the comfort factor of the wooden beaded contraption on his seat, consider transport and the pleasures of lubrication.

I give the driver a big tip for a small fare and ride the elevator I got stuck in this morning and fall into bed, fully dressed. The sheets will smell like me and someone else. The alarm won't wake me. The sun will rise, and I will be fast asleep.

BELIEF

While my cousin Donald, whom we all called Donny, was lying in a hospital bed at Lutheran General Hospital, a day and a half away from his death, my mother became convinced that she could heal him, wake him from his coma. It would be her presence at his bedside, her small jeweled and manicured hand in his, that would cause his eyes, which had been closed for two days with very little brain activity, to flutter open, graceful as an eel, and restore his consciousness and health.

She confided this to me, in a voice I didn't recognize as hers, shortly after Donny's death, while driving me home following a brunch with some cousins from her side of the family who were visiting from Florida. The dedication of Donny's headstone was a week away, and the event laid heavy as a boulder on my mother's chest.

Donny had only been dead for a little over two months, and while it was tradition to wait a full year before the dedication ceremony at the gravesite, his father and two brothers didn't want to prolong putting closure on Donny's life. Wasn't it enough of a strain, they argued, that he'd been sick for over three years? His death, to them, was a signal that he'd fought as long and hard as he could.

He never complained, my mother often said after visiting with him, never let on that he was experiencing any discomfort. My mother, who worked as a receptionist at a pediatrician's office in the medical center attached to the hospital, was a frequent visitor to Donny's bedside whenever he was hospitalized during his illness.

Donny was my father's nephew, the son of his eldest sister who had also died young, suddenly at age 57, of a brain aneurysm. Donny died less than a month away from his 34th birthday.

To say that my parents were closer to Donny than the children of any of my father's other siblings, would be a slight to those nieces and nephews. But Donny had worked for my father, as a salesclerk in his shoe store, for a few years after his divorce. Around the same time, he was renting an apartment near my parents' house and was a regular dinner guest. My sisters and I were all away at college, and having Donny around made the house seem less empty for my parents. My father had even offered Donny one of our vacant bedrooms, since we only came back for big holidays and we could all double up if we had to, and there was plenty of room.

Donny declined. He'd never lived alone. Growing up, he'd shared his bedroom with his younger brother. For the two years of college he'd attended at the University of Illinois at Champaign, he lived in a dorm room with two other guys. Then he'd met his future wife, whom he had lived with before they were married. He decided to try living by himself for awhile. He did, however, take my mother up on her frequent dinner invitations.

As a family, we believed we'd been lucky as far as death was concerned. Unlike other families we knew, we hadn't been faced with the deaths of many close relatives. No one had gone off to war and been killed. No drug overdoses, no tragic car crashes, no senseless deaths. Here and there were the traces of a bloodline strained by weak hearts. My father's father and his sister. My father's mother, afflicted with Multiple Sclerosis, lingered long in a wheelchair, all my memories of her set in a nursing home.

My mother believed she was luckiest of all, and she was. Both of her parents were still alive and in good health. One of her grandmothers had lived to be 92 years old. Both of her older brothers, one married and the other a confirmed bachelor, were also healthy, active and productive individuals.

Around the same time Donny became ill, my mother's best friend Carol was stricken with ovarian cancer. I remember her as a boisterous blonde, always laughing and telling stories about my mother's past. They'd grown up in the same north side neighborhood and went through school together, from kindergarten through high school.

Carol got married first, right after graduation, to a man she didn't love. He was a way out of her parents' dark and religiously orthodox home. They divorced after a year, and two weeks later Carol was maid of honor at my parents' wedding.

As a recently divorced woman, Carol was also an upstairs neighbor in the apartment building my parents moved into together in Albany Park, after they were married. The other women in Carol and my mother's social circle, their girlfriends, got married one right after the other. My mother was the first to become pregnant, with me, and she tells me that her friends received me as if I were royalty, especially Carol, who had found out that she was unable to have any children of her own.

Over the years, my mother's girlfriends married, started families and moved away from the city, out to the sprawling suburbs along Chicago's north shore. Carol had met someone, a doctor, who she fell in love with and married after a long and cautious courtship. They moved the farthest away, to Glencoe, and adopted three children.

My mother stayed close with her girlfriends and their families. Two of them had even settled in the same suburban village as my parents. The children attended each others' birthday parties. There were holiday picnics in the summer.

None of them were prepared for Carol's illness and swift decline. One of the women who had become estranged from the group took it especially hard. Since they had all been so close for so many years, they welcomed her back into the fold, and picked up with her where they had left off. The six women acted as nursemaids to Carol and her grief-stricken husband and children.

Carol participated in numerous experimental treatments and the spirits of my mother, and her girlfriends were lifted at the slightest indication of Carol rallying back to health. But, each of these successive improvements was met with a greater deterioration. Finally, after the most excruciating and extreme of the therapies, Carol died.

Her death had two very different effects on my mother. The first was to completely crush any faith she had in medical science. This caused a personal crisis for my mother, who, although she was not a doctor or nurse, was still employed in the medical field. She talked seriously about finding another job, in a different kind of office. My father and youngest sister talked her through this situation and in the end, she decided to keep her job.

The second result was that Carol's passing strengthened her resolve on seeing Donny through to complete recovery, by any means necessary. Much to my surprise, she had begun listening to the tapes of Louise Hay. I might have mentioned them to her at one time or another, that they'd been of some help to a friend of mine who had AIDS.

She spoke of crystals and their healing powers, all of which she'd read about in a book from the library. To my astonishment, she asked me if I would mind if she came with me to view the Names Project Quilt while it was on display at McCormick Place.

After we had parked the car in the underground lot, she remarked that she hoped there would be someone there to talk to, a surviving partner, a parent or relative, a caseworker. Someone who could offer her more than I could, since I was still having difficulty placing my grief after the death of my best friend, Raymond.

The Quilt experience was both good and bad for her. She was unprepared for the sheer size and scope of the display. The mixture of beauty and humor in the panels unsettled her. This was not the way she was accustomed to grieving. She was familiar with the dramatic mourning period of her religion and the cold, chiseled landscape of a cemetery.

On the other hand, she was encouraged by the people, friends and strangers alike, holding hands, holding each other in their arms, crying and somehow smiling through their tears.

I'm not sure what the overall outcome was. She had spoken to a few people that day, and revealed that even though Donny didn't have AIDS, she could honestly empathize with their losses. Cancer patients, she noted, sounding like she had also been recently reading Sontag, were once treated as outcasts in much the same way people with AIDS are presently dealt with by society.

Somewhere, my mother was able to find what she needed to fortify her belief. Up until the very last minute of Donny's life, my mother seemed to give off a glow of conviction as if it were some kind of life force.

I was not so fortunate. I had all but eliminated the words belief and faith from my vocabulary. Nothing was immune; not the government, organized religion, medicine or even, love.

It wasn't until a chest of drawers that had belonged to Donny ended up in my possession, on my parents' insistence, that I began to start believing, again.

Because of conflicting schedules and bad weather, the dresser sat in my parents' garage for almost two months between the time it was removed from Donny's condo in Schaumburg and brought to my apartment in the city. On that day, I emptied out the small chest of drawers that I'd had since I was a child. I was a little torn, at first, about parting with the nicked and scratched mahogany dresser, being something of a packrat and somewhat sentimental. For example, knowing my penchant for collecting things, my parents offered to return the signed copy of my book of poems that I had given to Donny during the longest and last of his hospital stays. My mother told me that he had kept it on his nightstand at the hospital. He had even asked her to read to him from the book. He was a big fan of my work, which pleasantly surprised and flattered me. I'd never thought of him as much of a devotee of poetry. The Chicago White Sox and the Bears were more his style. I guess I was wrong about Donny.

I had moved the empty, old dresser out into the hallway, and onto the elevator, meeting my father on the street in front of my apartment building. He was unloading Donny's dresser from his van. It was quite a bit taller and wider than my old one. For a moment, I worried that it wouldn't fit into the space the old dresser had occupied in my studio apartment.

My mother was there, too, an expression of quiet contemplation on her face. She guarded the van, as if anybody would want to steal the old dresser, while my father and I struggled with Donny's dresser, on a hand truck, up the two concrete steps and into the building's entrance. We managed to fit it into the small elevator and then wheeled it into the apartment and into place. It fit remarkably well, and my father looked pleased.

I saw my father to the door and asked him to kiss my mother goodbye for me. I went to look for an old dust rag with which to wipe off the chest of drawers. The clothes that had been in the old dresser, underwear, socks, silk-screened t-shirts, belts and suspenders were strewn on my bed.

I opened the top drawer of the dresser and discovered that someone, Donny I suppose, had lined the drawers with contact paper patterned with a cartoonish jungle scene. Lions, tigers, giraffes, elephants, monkeys and palm trees. This made me smile for a moment and I even laughed, recalling Donny's taste in corny jokes.

Then, when I least expected to have my faith renewed, I opened the second drawer. Scattered across the brown, black and white wild animals of the contact paper lining were six pennies and an old fortune cookie fortune that read "Someday, your name will be famous." And from that moment on, I believed.

BULLY IN A BAR

The night started out like this: badly. I had agreed to meet some friends for dinner at a trendy restaurant on the near north side. My best friend, Jody, had won tickets to a comedy club called Laughing Stock and that's where we were heading after we ate. Jody was excited about seeing the headlining comedian's performance because he had a crush on him.

Rumor had it that he was gay and those were the two things Jody thrived on: rumors and gay men. Jody himself had tried his hand at stand-up comedy and failed. Luckily, he didn't quit his day-job, managing a movie memorabilia store in Oak Park. The few times he did perform, we were there, all ten of us, to give him moral support. His humor was kind of dark and probably insulted more than a few people.

My favorite bit of his was a routine he did about the far south suburbs of Chicago. He was born and raised on the North Shore, in Wilmette, and somewhere in his upbringing a total dislike of anything south of the city had been instilled. I was from the north side of Chicago myself and shared some of his feelings, but I couldn't match his intensity or his wit.

I'm trying to think of how it went. Oh, yeah. He would start it by saying, "Do you know what the worst thing about living in Chicago is?" Then he'd pause and let the audience mull it over, but not too long. He didn't want them to think his act had anything to do with audience participation. He'd say, "Indiana." That usually got him some laughs and then he would proceed to annihilate the suburbs near the Illinois/Indiana border.

He started off with Harvey. He'd say, "Harvey. Who the hell wants to live in a town named after a six-foot invisible rabbit? And what about Hazel Crest, a town dedicated to Shirley Booth and a tube of toothpaste? Do the residents

74

of Joliet stand on their balconies calling out 'Romeoville, Romeoville, wherefore art thou Romeoville?'"

By that point I'd be doubled over in laughter, my eyes tearing. I'd heard the jokes so many times, I could almost recite them myself, but there was something in his delivery; a combination of malice and affection.

Then he'd say, "If people from Homewood are Homewoodians, are people from Flossmoor Flossmorons? What about nearby Riverdale? Isn't that where Archie, Veronica, Betty and Jughead are from? Don't get me started on Stinkney, I mean Stickney, home of the sewage treatment plant. On a clear day you can see Cicero." And so on.

It was most definitely local humor. Unfortunately, some of the locals didn't take too kindly to Jody's rampages and word got around that he was a must to avoid. I don't think they gave him a fair chance. He had just started writing some new material on the city's neighborhoods that was a stitch. But Jody was a good sport and ended that brief chapter of his professional life. He still makes me laugh and I love him for it.

Jody also knew what buttons to push to make me mad. Livid was a better word. His fascination with rumors, the creation, spreading, and results of rumors, bordered on obsession. I could probably count on one hand the number of times he hadn't begun a sentence with, "Guess what I heard today?" What he usually didn't say was that he'd heard it from his own mouth and was just now getting to the task of launching it, like some space shuttle, into orbit somewhere above the atmosphere.

Picture this: a lazy Saturday afternoon at the beginning of fall. Some remnants of summer still can be found, but Walmart's back-to-school sale had been in full swing for a couple of weeks by this time. The grade school across the street from where I lived hummed with the sound of returning students, uncooperative after a brief but liberating summer. I couldn't help but feel some sympathy for those kids.

I hated school. Not so much the learning part as the social aspect. I couldn't do it. It wasn't until years later, sitting in my therapist's office that I understood. It had something to do with being different from my fellow classmates, but not knowing how or why. I was your average, run-of-the-mill misfit. You know, the last one picked for any athletic team, the one who got excused from participating in gym at the first sign of the slightest sniffle or chill, the walking punching-bag.

The few friends I had were in the same boat as I was, and we stayed friends for many years, several of us coming out to each other in high school or college when we had a better grasp of the situation, so to speak.

Jody, who was a few years younger than me, had had an easier time. Things had changed by the time he was in high school and he even had the honor of organizing the school district's first gay student club. For some reason, we avoided talking about school, unless it was college, where I finally found a place to fit in.

Back to September. I had just finished cleaning the apartment (a Saturday ritual), when the phone rang.

"OK," Jody said instead of hello, "here's the plan. We're meeting at Freddy's at 5:45. We can go in two cars since there's eight of us. Brian's not coming because he and Mitch had a fight and he wants to stay home and sulk. Cole is probably going to meet us at the restaurant, but he's not sure if he's going to the comedy club. He said something about a full moon party somewhere. Anyway, the attire is casual, but not too. Got all that?"

I was quiet for a moment, trying to let it all sink in. It was a moment too many.

"You there, or what?" Jody asked.

"I'm here," I said. "Where are you?"

"At the shop. It's dead today, which is good because I want to have some energy for tonight. I met someone who knows Benny's agent. And he's agreed to get me a private audience with him."

"Benny?" I asked, regretting it the moment I said it.

"Where have you been? Kansas? Benny, the comedian we're going to see tonight. Benny the Boner? Snap out of it, kid. What's-his-name's not coming back. We're going out tonight, remember? To get your mind off him."

What's-his-name was Willie, my ex. We'd recently broken up after being together for three years and I was still a little blue. Time does not permit me to go into detail. Just let me say that I loved him and miss him terribly. Jody had taken it upon himself to help me forget Willie, but he still had a long way to go.

"Besides, I saw him and his new beau last night at the Condom Nation party at Vortex and they looked dreamily happy."

"New beau?" I said. "Gee, that was fast."

"Oh, come on," Jody said, "two weeks is not fast."

"I wonder how long he would have waited if I'd died, instead of broken up with him. He probably wouldn't even have observed a proper mourning period."

"Black is not his color," Jody said. "And besides, you said it yourself, you broke up with him."

It was true. I had initiated the breakup. But it was only because I thought he had wanted it, too. And here I was, feeling lonely and depressed about something for which I was fully responsible. Like seeing a brick wall and making the decision to try and drive through it, instead of around. It's just that hearing about Willie and someone else had turned my mood sour.

"Tell me about him," I said. Then, "No. Don't. I don't want to know."

"Well," Jody said, having only heard the first part and accepting the invitation, "someone told me that he's a bike messenger in the Loop by day and a DJ in some leather club by night. From the looks of him, I'd believe it. The boy has serious Michelangelo features. Sculpted to the nines. And not a hair on his body. Someone told me that he's naturally smooth, but I think he shaves...."

"Enough," I said, "I don't want to hear anymore."

"Wait, it gets better. Supposedly they met through one of those computer bulletin board services. That's just like Willie, isn't it? Here we are going out on the prowl publicly and he's got himself sequestered in front of his computer playing gay nineties Nintendo or something. I heard that he does all his 'computer-dating' at work. But that could be just a rumor."

"Shut the fuck up, Jody. I mean it. I don't want to hear another word."

"Well, I...Okay," he said, acquiescing. "None of this is fact, anyway. I mean I saw them together, and I mean together, and I just assumed...."

"Count me out tonight," I said, certain that that was the only way to end the conversation and get Jody's attention at the same time. Jody was uncharacteristically quiet. I could hear him breathing. We lingered for a few seconds in a cloud of silence. Just as I was about to hang up, Jody sneezed.

"Bless you," I said out of reflex.

"Thank you," he said, "although I'm not the one who needs to be blessed. Listen, I know you're going through a rough patch, but if there's anything I can do to make it easier...."

"You can start by saying goodbye, then hanging up."

"You'll be missed," Jody said, "more than you know. Goodbye."

I should have stayed home, but I couldn't. I felt like I had been possessed by one of those demons you read about on the cover of the tabloids at supermarket check-out stands. I looked at myself in the mirror and immediately started getting undressed. I had to shave, shower, pick out something to wear. It's a pity that my pith helmet was in for repairs, I was going to need it for my night of hunting.

According to the local club directory, I had three leather bars to choose from. One was an old standard, moved to a new location. The other two were newer, in a different part of the city altogether. It was still early enough that I could take a nap, rest up, before I ventured out to all three in geographical order.

This is what I wore: faded Levi 501's with rips in strategic places, a t-shirt with a Keith Haring print on it, black motorcycle boots and a black leather motorcycle jacket with lacing on the side. I'd never taken this "uniform" seriously before. I didn't own a motorcycle and had only ridden on one once, hanging on to the driver as if he were a rock jutting out of a cliff I'd just fallen over.

It was simply a costume, an outfit. A get-up to get off in. I came out at the end of the clone era. There were still a few flannel shirts in my closet, but I had thrown out my work boots two winters before when I discovered holes in both soles. The jeans I wore had been a part of my wardrobe for as long as I could remember, signifying nothing more than my desire for comfort and leisure.

For me, leather had always had more to do with style than sex. I had thought Willie felt the same way when we bought our matching jackets. After the recent series of events, I realized that I had been mistaken.

In the car, on the way to the first bar, I remembered that I forgot to turn the answering machine on. Not that there had been any messages left, of interest, recently. For awhile, I'd gotten what I called, a "breather." He didn't breathe so much as chant. The litany of the caller consisted of a list of things he wanted to do to me in his cellar, which he referred to as his "dungeon."

The first time he called, right after Willie and I broke up, I had thought it was Willie. Drunk or stoned, I thought he was trying to reveal a side of himself that he had kept hidden during our relationship. The caller spoke in a loud whisper and recited the same list each time he called. One time, I picked up the phone and started to encourage him. I told him that I would love the chance to be shackled to the wall and force-fed his kielbasa. That I wouldn't mind playing with each one of his cornucopia of sex toys and latex novelties. That I wouldn't have a problem vacuuming his apartment with my feet bound, hands handcuffed to the Hoover. But that I would have to draw the line at rolling around in molasses with his Great Dane and Rottweiler.

He stopped groaning in agreement and said, "Hey wait a minute, is this Tony? Is this 555-1555?"

And before I had a chance to answer, he hung up and hadn't called back since. I drove around the block a couple of times when I got to the bar, but there was no place to park. The neighborhood was residential, a combination of Hispanics and Koreans and assorted eastern European immigrants, and I wondered what they thought about the men dressed in black leather going in and out of the corner bar across from Wendy's Hamburgers. Finally, I opted to park in the Wendy's lot, since I had seen other men doing it and then going into the bar.

Walking into the bar was like entering a vegetarian's worst nightmare. Even the patrons themselves were packed in like cattle. I weaved my way through, staying close to the wall which was spray-painted with designer graffiti. Generic disco music played so loud that conversation was limited. I turned a quick corner and was in the backroom. Two video screens were showing leather porn, men with overly muscled bodies tugging on each other's nipple rings, spanking each other and shooting gallons of cum at the camera.

When I ordered a drink at the bar, I asked the bartender where the DJ sat. He pointed to an elevated booth near the entrance to the backroom. I paid for my beer and walked over to a crowded corner. A young man with bleached blonde hair, wearing leather chaps, a harness and a studded leather jock smiled at me.

"Welcome to the geriatric ward," he said. "You look too young to be back here."

"You too," I said, "or else you hide your age well."

"I'm looking for a daddy," he said. "What's your excuse?"

"I'm looking for..." I started to say, then changed my mind. "I'm looking for a friend."

"What's his name?"

"I'm not sure," I said.

"Well," he said, "if I run into him, I'll tell him you're looking for him."

"Thanks," I said, and walked away.

I really had no idea that there were so many men into this scene. Most of them were draped from head to toe in leather. Some of the men in the backroom were shirtless in keeping with the bar's policy of "leather or skin only" in the backroom. Everyone in the backroom seemed to be staring at some point in space just over my head or to the left or right. A friend once told me that eye contact with the wrong person in a leather bar could lead to long hours of unexpected pain or pleasure. Since no one met my gaze, I felt safe. In fact, I felt like I'd just stumbled into a Helmut Newton photo shoot. S and M, I thought. Stand and model.

I eased my way to the DJ booth. A fat man in lederhosen was at the turntable. He had a long, full black beard and no mustache. His left ear was dotted with rhinestone studs from the lobe to the top. I tried to imagine Willie being attracted to someone like this and then I remembered Jody's description. No match. Game over. Try again.

The DJ turned the music down and talked into a microphone.

"In ten minutes, it's show time. Hot Rod will be here with his amazing muscle puppets to entertain and abuse, I mean amuse you. So, stay where you are, have another drink and don't forget to tip the bartenders, you cheap bastards."

He laughed and pushed a button on the console to make it echo and fade and then the music came back louder than before.

This DJ was no bike messenger. He was no comedian either. So, I finished my beer and left. Two police cars raced up Clark Street, their blue strobe lights flashing, sirens screaming. I'd have to limit my beer consumption. I was in no mood to deal with Chicago's men in blue.

I decided to pass on the bar located in between the first one and the third. I knew that finding street parking would be more of a challenge than I was up to. As luck would have it, parking near the Hot Tin Roof was just as frustrating. Patience won out, though, and I found a spot right in front. Convinced that my luck was about to change, I took this as a sign from above.

Movement inside the bar was limited to short, sideways steps. If the first bar was like a cattle car, then I knew I'd arrived in Sardine City. Right away, I sensed that the crowd was different. Younger, more attractive, more hardcore. I couldn't tell if the group of men standing outside the open door to the bathroom was a line to get in, to observe, or just standing there for lack of a better place.

The room in the middle, where the pool table and coat check were, was less crowded, but not much. Muscled leathermen wielding pool cues circled the table as if it were that night's sex partner. Beer bottles were lined up along the pool table's edge.

To say that the backroom was dark would be like saying that Millie Bush was a pampered pet. The small video screen on the wall over the bar casts insufficient light. The high intensity lights in the ceiling were turned down to the dimmest possible level without being completely off. I didn't see so much as feel my way to the first available open space against a wall.

Was this place really Willie's style? I wondered. Darker and gloomier than the other bars we frequented when we were together. The DJ's musical selections ran more towards industrial music than the fluffy dance songs Willie and I liked to dance to. Could this DJ be Willie's latest?

The bar-back squeezed by with a tub full of dirty glasses.

"Hey," I yelled, "where's the DJ sit?"

"Don't ask me why he plays this shit," he said, "why don't you ask him yourself?"

And then he walked away, hoisting the grey rubber tub over his head. I felt a little embarrassed, as if everyone around me had overheard our confused exchange. I decided to scout him out myself. I walked to the back end of the back room, near another bathroom, where a group of men had squeezed themselves into the darkest part of the bar. At first, I thought they were dancing. Then someone grabbed my wrist and directed it to his exposed dick. Still holding my wrist, he closed my hand around it. I could smell poppers. Another man lit a cigarette and in the brief light of the match, I could see that everyone was involved in some sex act or another. I let go of this stranger and walked as fast as I could back to the front room of the bar.

I ordered a drink to calm my nerves. It was then that I saw him. Not the DJ, whom I had hoped to locate and bag for the evening. It was someone else. Someone that I hadn't seen for a long time. Someone I knew I'd never forget.

He didn't recognize me. I could tell by the way he stared vacantly past me. There was no glimmer of recognition or familiarity. Of course, I didn't look the same. I was taller and my hair was darker than it had been. My body was bulkier, solid after years at the gym. Shoulders, broad and wide, narrowing down my torso to my thirty-one-inch waist. The tag on the back of my 501's read thirty-six-inch inseam, but it was really only thirty-five.

I recognized him right away, leaning against the bar at Hot Tin Roof. He still wore his hair the same way he did then. It was cut short on the sides and back, curly and full on top. His body was still the brick-solid mass it had been all through school. I remembered him towering over me, throughout our youth, and now I had to look down a little to take him all in. I looked down into his eyes from halfway across the dimly lit bar and knew for sure that it was him.

Those eyes, that vacant stare, could only belong to one person. Sage Nichols. Sage Nichols, who with one blink of those empty eyes could turn half the boys on the playground into a quivering assemblage of Jell-O and the other half against you. Sage Nichols, feared by educators, clergymen, parents, laborers, eighty-nine percent of the suburban village's population where we had grown up.

Now, if you would have asked me what my greatest sexual fantasy was, I wouldn't have hesitated for a minute to tell you. For years, I scoured the gay bars in search of childhood bullies. You know, the guys who had some magical insight into your future. The ones who helped to cement your role in society without the slightest provocation. Not that I believe that being gay has anything to do with environment. Oh no, DNA is more powerful than any menace in a little league uniform. I searched for these bullies, in gay bars, because if they knew I was queer, then they must have known that they were queer, too.

I was right, too. I must have run into half of the varsity football and wrestling teams during my first few years of going out to the bars. A couple of the MVP baseball players from my high school are now outfielders with the gay softball league. Never having spent more time in a high school locker room than necessary, I would imagine that there was some heavy male bonding going on in the showers. Maybe there was something in the water.

Running into Sage Nichols at one of the city's premiere leather bars felt like the culmination and rich reward of some complex sociological experiment. I considered preparing my Nobel Prize acceptance speech for a moment and then put it on hold until I completed my research.

"I'll have a Coors," I said to the bartender who was wearing a dyed black jockstrap.

When he brought me my beer, I asked what Sage was drinking.

"Black Russians," he said, "since he got here."

"Been here long?" I asked.

"Couple of hours," he said.

I gave him a twenty.

"Keep them coming," I said.

I turned away from the bar and scanned the room, my eyes stopping on a man with red hair and a nose ring. Behind him, a man with a Mohawk, wearing black bicycle shorts, no shirt and a leather jacket, pushed his way past, heading for the backroom.

"Someone's in a hurry," I heard Sage say.

"He must be late for a very important date," I said, turning to face him.

"Thanks," he said, raising his glass.

"Don't mention it," I said. "And that's, 'Thanks, Sir.'"

"'Thanks, Sir,'" he repeated and downed the drink.

I don't know what came over me. Sir? I wondered if "sir" was a far cry from crying uncle. I was willing to find out.

"Been in back?" I asked.

"Not my scene," he said, "uh, Sir."

"Oh, really?" I asked. "From the looks of you, I thought a big guy like yourself could have a good time back there."

"Yes and no...Sir. I like one on one better."

Sure, I thought, without his gang of thugs, he was a pussy. He turned to face me full front, adjusting his basket. Impressive, but I couldn't let him see that I was interested too soon. He beat me to it. "You live alone? Around here? Sir?"

"Not far," I said. "What about you?"

"A few blocks. I walked over."

"Live alone?"

"Me and my lizard."

Lizard? I thought. Is Sage still playing word games? Was his lizard a pet or a pet name for his dick?

"Does the lizard have a name?"

"Hector," he said and grinned a mouthful of perfect suburban teeth.

"You got a name?" I asked, fighting back the urge to say it when he did.

"Sage, Sir. Like the spice."

"Nice to meet you, Sage," I said extending a hand cold from holding the beer. "You can call me...Sir."

"The pleasure is all mine, Sir. Or it could be."

"It could," I said, "if you play your cards right."

"I hope we're talking about something a little more exciting than Bridge or Old Maid here, Sir."

"How are you at Poker?" I asked.

"It all depends on what I'm dealt, Sir."

"I promise not to stack the deck," I said. Not too badly, I thought.

And then he moved closer, pulling me to him with an arm as quick and strong as a tentacle. We breathed into each other's faces; eyes locked. He was solid as a man-mountain. His hand moved down my lower back to the seat of my jeans. He found one of the rips below the left back pocket and inserted his hand. He closed his mouth and breathed through his nose. His eyes were brown and empty as his glass.

I didn't know what to do with my arms. He added pressure to his hand in my jeans and our crotches met, both hard and warm. I put my hands on his shoulders and squeezed. I stopped myself from putting them around his throat. Plenty of time, I thought.

"Take me home. Now, Sir."

Sage lived on a street that was mostly single-family homes. His apartment building, in the middle of the block, stood out like an unhealthy tree in a forest. He lived in a garden apartment that was sparsely furnished. A futon, some stereo equipment, a Soloflex machine. There were dirty dishes in the sink. The hardwood floors looked like they'd just been swept. The television was on, volume turned down, and the light on his answering machine was flashing. A referee's shirt was hanging on a hook on the back of the front door.

"You a ref?" I asked, the first words either of us had spoken since we'd left the bar.

"Gym teacher," he said.

Of course, I almost said out loud. Sage Nichols oversees training the next generation of jock bullies.

"In the city?"

"No, Sir. At the high school I graduated from, in the 'burbs.'"

I thought he had dropped out. I didn't remember him at graduation. It was probably because I had a crush on the valedictorian and had blocked out everything else from that day. As he answered that question, he was getting undressed. I noticed a tub of lube and a box of Trojans on the floor next to the futon. He wasn't wearing anything under the black Levi's. I was still dressed, watching him, looking around the apartment with only the light from the television.

He walked a few steps over to me and slid my jacket off, dropping it on the floor. I helped him lift the t-shirt over my head. He wrapped his arms around me, giving me a bear hug. My boots left the ground. He pressed his face into my chest. I could feel the stubble on his cheeks and chin. I grabbed his head, my fingers in his hair, and pulled back. His eyes seemed to have changed color, as if someone had turned on a light inside his head. He lowered me a bit, tried to kiss me, but I just pulled his head back, further away.

We released each other. He got on his knees and popped the buttons on my jeans, sliding them down to the top of my boots. He moved backwards, still on his knees, towards the futon. We were separated only by the length of my hard-on. Sage eased himself onto his back. He reached under the edge of the futon and pulled out a pair of handcuffs.

"Please, Sir, if you would do the honors."

This was going to be easier than I had thought. At the head of the futon was a radiator, still cold in September. I raised his hands over his head, putting the right cuff on first, then the left, threading the chain around one of the legs of the radiator.

His legs and his torso were muscular, but not grotesque. At some point he must have taken the time to develop his body beyond the point of just bulk. His legs and chest were dusted with dark hair, although his stomach was bare and flat. He had an average-sized dick and low-hanging balls.

He rocked gently from side to side on the futon, as if there were a rhythm track playing in his head. And then he flipped over onto his stomach. He half-stifled a grunt. The handcuffs must have been cutting into his wrist, but there had to have been enough give in the links for him to make that kind of move.

His ass, lit up by a late-night movie on the television, was hairless, smooth and domed. He turned his head, breathing into his arm pit.

"My legs, Sir," he said.

"They're nice," I said. "What about them?"

"Under the right corner of the futon, Sir. There's some Velcro-restraints. There are places to fasten them near where you're kneeling."

I lifted the right corner and there they were. They were a little bent and I tried to straighten them out. While I did, Sage spread his legs slightly, pointed with his toes to where the restraints could be fastened on the futon.

"You do this yourself?" I asked.

"No, Sir. A friend of mine did it. He did the same thing to his."

I unfastened the restraints and slid them over his feet and around his ankles. I started to tighten the left one.

"Make it tight. So I can't move too much."

"Oh, I intend to," I said, fighting back the urge to giggle.

When the restraints were around both ankles and fastened to the futon, I stood up. My knees cracked. I looked down at my erection. It was so hard it hurt. I shuffled over to the television, jeans around my calves. I picked up the remote control and began changing channels.

"What are you doing, Sir?"

"I'm looking for the weather channel," I said.

"Please, Sir, don't make me wait. I want it now. I've been very bad and I need to be punished. You can punish me, can't you, Sir?"

"That depends on how bad you've been," I said. "How bad have you been, Sage?"

"Real bad, Sir. Worse than you can imagine."

"Oh, I don't know," I said, "I have a pretty vivid imagination. And a pretty good memory, too."

"A pretty good memory, Sir? I don't get it."

"Oh, you will," I said.

There was an old Jerry Lewis/Dean Martin movie on. It looked like it had been colorized. Jerry Lewis was mugging for the camera. Dean Martin rolled his eyes. I turned off the TV.

"I don't remember you being at the graduation ceremonies, Sage. Didn't you drop out?"

"The graduation ceremonies?" he asked. His voice a little uncertain.

"Yeah, graduation. Class of '76. Remember? Red, white and blue tassels?"

"I wasn't there," he said.

"I wasn't there, Sir," I said.

"I wasn't there, Sir," he echoed. "I was expelled. I wasn't allowed to participate. I had to repeat my senior year in the fall. Then I dropped out."

"You never graduated from high school, Sage?"

"I got my GED."

He had started to rock slightly. If he wanted to turn over onto his back, he'd have a hard time. The Velcro-restraints were tight. He'd have to roll, uncross his wrists, then cross his legs at an awkward angle.

I pulled my jeans up over my hard-on. I picked up my t-shirt and slipped it over my head. The leather jacket was still on the floor where we'd left it. I walked over to the side of the futon in the direction where Sage's head was turned.

"I graduated from high school," I said, "first try. If you had been at graduation, you would have known I was second in the class. I also graduated Cum Laude from college. I did those things despite you. In fact, I think I owe you a word of thanks. You managed to keep me off most playing fields and out of most social circles, so I had the time to study and get good grades, make the honor roll. So, thank you."

"Who are you?" he asked, his voice poised between fear and excitement.

"Who are you, Sir?" I snapped.

"Who the fuck are you?" he responded, a new edge in his tone. "Sir?"

"Names are not important," I said. "So, don't even bother guessing. Let's just say I'm one of the many."

"Many?"

"Many victims. Recipients of Sage's 'flaming fist'. You remember the 'flaming fist', don't you, Sage?"

"Vaguely...Sir," he said and hesitated. "Maybe you could refresh my memory."

"Yeah," I said, "you'd like that, wouldn't you? Payback is a bitch, isn't it, Sage?"

"Let me up," he said, "Sir."

"You give, Sage? You giving up? And not a bruise or broken blood vessel or cracked rib on you. Not a scratch. Sage walks away unharmed again. The champ of the school yard."

"Let me up," he said, again, but louder.

I dropped to my knees, inches from his face. He flinched.

"What's the matter, Sage? Scared that I might hurt you. The night isn't long enough for me to hurt you the way you should be hurt. No, I'll be satisfied if I can just wound your ego. Leave a scar."

And then I grabbed his face with both hands and kissed him on the mouth. Our tongues jabbed at each other. My lips stung and I was afraid to check them, see if they'd been split. I couldn't taste blood, just alcohol. While I held his head, I turned mine, making sure to cover every inch of his mouth with mine. We both breathed loudly through our noses. The smacking noise echoed throughout the room. His eyes were open, and I looked into them. They were moist. I tasted one of his tears as it rolled down his cheek, onto mine and into our kiss. I stopped. His mouth was still open, not satisfied. A big, hungry, baby boy.

"Where's the key?" I asked.

"Key?"

"To the handcuffs."

"Top right-hand drawer in the kitchen."

I walked away from him. He was breathing hard, panting. I turned the light on in the kitchen. A cold, white fluorescent bulb buzzed over my head. I found the key and went back to Sage. He watched me approach, my face in shadow, lit from behind. I lifted the screen in the open window above the radiator. I threw the key out the window.

"What the fuck did you do that for?"

"Payback is a bitch," I said. "In a few days, you'll probably lose enough weight to slip right out of those."

I walked into the kitchen and turned off the light. Back in the living room, I turned off the answering machine. Sage watched me and then dropped his head between his extended arms. He cried softly into the futon.

"Don't cry, Sage," I said, "only sissies cry. Isn't that what you used to tell me? Take it like a man and all that bullshit. What would the guys in the bar or the boys on the wrestling team think?"

His shoulders shook. I was surprisingly aroused. I could have dropped my pants and fucked him right there. It was a real Kodak moment. I took a picture in my mind, framed it and put it on the mantlepiece. I called it "Blubbering Bully."

A DIFFERENT DEBRA

Debra, when I first met you, you liked women. You had a girlfriend named Patti who lived in the city, in the narrow "Cigarette Pack" house on Montana. Her father was a Chicago cop and he disapproved. She was tough and intimidating the way you imagine the teenage lesbian daughter of a cop would be. She was the last remnant of your urban life.

Here's the excuse your newly widowed mother used to move you and your three younger sisters out of the house you grew up in near the intersection of Ashland and Pratt in East Rogers Park into a suburban townhouse that was half the size, overlooking Jamaican Gardens and the Edens Expressway: the old neighborhood was becoming unsafe. What she meant by that was that, while the old house was in disrepair and your father's meager life insurance policy paid for his funeral and burial at Calvary Cemetery and not much else and there was evidence of a migration of families from the South Side to the North Side, and there were muggings and other crimes being perpetrated (not unlike what was happening in other parts of the city from the lakefront to the western border). What she meant was that she thought it was dangerous the way Patti snuck in and out of your first-floor bedroom window at all hours of the night and day, never using the front door, ever.

Skokie was too much for us. We ran to the city any way we could. By bus – the 97 to the 151 or 36 – or train – the Skokie Swift to the Howard L – when my car – a crumbling bright blue Plymouth Gold Duster – couldn't be trusted. When it worked, we'd fly down Lake Shore Drive, twist and roll on Sheridan Road and Broadway, or descend Clark Street from its Chicago Avenue roots in Evanston.

The radio was our soundtrack, our backing band. The hippie DJs at WXRT almost never played the new wave we craved, but occasionally they would shock us with something by Elvis Costello, the Ramones, Blondie, Talking Heads, the Clash or Television. We rolled the windows down and howled our anthems to the moon. We never listened to WLUP - The Loop - because Styx and the Doobie Brothers and Foreigner made us want to drive into oncoming traffic, straight into Lake Michigan.

We hated Martin. Maybe that's too strong a word. We couldn't figure out why Martin was in love with me. Stumped, I say. He was so physically hot that he had those mirage waves, the kind you sometimes see on the street in the summer, all around him. His curly hair shimmered and his Roman nose, his deep dimples and cleft chin begged to be incorporated into every kiss.

Martin was a dancer. His body said what his mouth fell dumb to, what his hands couldn't spell. We alternated dancing vertically and horizontally. His sinewy arms and broad shoulders, muscular legs and firm pecs and tight, flat stomach, smooth and solid butt, were meant to be in motion, never at rest; leaping through the air, in and out of the front seat of my car, zipping and buttoning his jeans as he went.

His awkwardness, however, wasn't a mirage. He should have been chasing after attainable boys in his own age, attractiveness and physical appearance bracket. We devoted hours to calculating and debating what he could possibly see in a skinny, moody, indecisive, punk rock guy like me. We came up empty-handed.

The night I met you, Debra, it was August and cool. We were on either side of the bookstore counter. I worked days as an assistant branch manager at the Bank of Skokie, and nights I manned the cash register at the Magazine Rack in the strip mall next to the train station. It kept me out of and away from my parents' house, where I was doing penance for quitting college.

You were part of Steve and Gordy's shadow. They forgot to introduce us that night, so I reached out a hand and said my name. You grasped it and said, "Enchanted," and I was. They had just picked you up from work, Edward's in Old Orchard, where you waited tables for tips and minimum wage, and wrote poems on napkins and the backs of order pads. You looked like trouble and I was looking for trouble.

I was an object of desire that brutal summer. Martin took care of business with Steve and Gordy and the boys outside. No use upsetting me, fragile as I was. I was his. He would never come between you and me. We talked incessantly about books and writers. We were poets. We knew how to make words jerk and snap, vibrate, or stand perfectly still.

We all danced; clumsy, un-choreographed, with abandon, exposing ourselves without ever getting undressed. Every night began and ended in men's bars where you sometimes weren't welcome, given the third degree by the bouncer. "Do you know what kind of bar this is? Do you have six more forms of ID?" Once inside, we'd find my friends who adored you, craved the sound of your voice, your laugh, devoured your smile like a drug.

Every song was declared our favorite and we danced to all of them. Disco Demolition be damned, we loved the nightlife and the "disco 'round." Each dance was a slow dance when you and Patti danced together on the illuminated or wood parquet-tiled or slippery linoleum dancefloors of the various nightclubs we frequented. Beats per minute slowed to a crawl. Everyone around you jumped and bumped, stepped and leapt, kicked their heels and flicked their wrists, but the two of you never ceased the slo-mo torso grind, the dance step you claimed to have invented. Drenched in our own fluids, we rested just long enough to regain our strength, filing onto the dance floor, renewed and vital.

Do you remember how you "saved my life" one night, Debra? You sat hunched and fetal in the front seat of my car in the parking lot of Charlie's Angels. Forcing yourself to cry, you looked desperate, suicidal, so I wouldn't have to go home with the two men I'd met at a party. We drove away, doubled over in spasms of laughter and relief. Imagine me, one-third of a threesome. It was the summer after Gacy. Secretly, I imagined them killing me, burying me in a crawlspace, sealing me in a wall of their house.

When you visited me in Providence, where I had moved to return to college, you seemed changed. By then, you and Patti had been broken up for a few months. The reasons were vague, the details not forthcoming. You got a job at Bank of Skokie, on my recommendation. When we talked about the staff, laughing and making fun of the same people, you kept dropping the name of one of the loan officers. You didn't laugh. Sure, I remembered him. Yes, he was handsome in his dark, three-piece suits and polished shoes; his dark blonde hair and thick mustache. His large class ring glistening in the fluorescent light of the lobby. His red Camaro parked in the same spot of the parking lot, every season, during banking hours.

A year later, when the wedding invitation arrived, I wasn't surprised. I knew that people changed like the weather. But I missed the other Debra. The one who admirably exercised control with patchouli. The Debra who fell partway into a sewer the day we went to say goodbye to Martin before I moved away, losing one platform clog, but gaining a tetanus shot. The one who smoked Eve menthol cigarettes all the way to the filter. The Debra who alphabetized and itemized what it was that women did together in bed, solving a mystery I would have rather left uncovered. The one who wanted to go out dancing every night during her first and only visit to Providence, to see how things compared to Chicago.

I had no choice but to accept the fact that that Debra was gone for good. I held the proof in my hands. It took every ounce of self-control I had not to call you and ask you what happened to the other Debra, where she went, if she was ever coming back. It took every cell of my dignity not to ask if you had invited Martin to the wedding, too.

THE LONG WAY HOME

Ira called the number Jason had given him twice a day, every day, for the first week after the night they met at Pepper's. This was in 1979, before everyone had answering machines. Ira would let the phone ring a dozen or more times before hanging up. He had decided that six rings were usually enough to wake someone up if they were asleep. Eight rings were enough to allow someone who had been in the shower enough time to grab a towel and get to the phone. Ten rings were satisfactory if someone was just getting in the door with an armload of groceries. Twelve rings were a courtesy. Anything more was just to fuck with luck.

At twenty, Ira had been sexually active for at least five years, but he never went home with anyone from a bar. He had, however, a few years earlier, gotten a blow job in the men's bathroom at Water Tower Place, from a man who cruised him at the Rizzoli Bookstore and then persuaded Ira to follow him into a stall. Ira had even gone so far as to board a northbound CTA bus with the man but lost his nerve after two stops and ran out the back door.

A few months after his Water Tower Place sexual rendezvous, Ira encountered a man in a forest-green velvet suit on LaSalle Street who convinced him to follow him into one of the men's bathrooms at the Merchandise Mart. In the stall, the man crouched down, careful not to let his velvet suit touch the floor, and sucked Ira off. He gave Ira a piece of paper with his name, "Roy," and phone number scrawled on it.

Ira called him a month later. When he asked for Roy, the man who answered said that he had the wrong number. Ira hung up and dialed the number again. The same man answered, and this time asked Ira his name. They started to have a polite conversation, and then the man revealed that he was, in fact, the same one who had picked Ira up on LaSalle Street. His name was Ben Royal, and "Roy" was the name, he said, that he gave to his tricks. He asked Ira to describe himself, and Ira said that he was about five feet ten, with dishwater blonde hair and a reddish beard.

"I remember you," Ben said, "you're the skinny college boy with the big dick, right?"

Ira didn't know what to say. No one had ever described him that way before.

"You gave me a blow job at the Merchandise Mart," Ira said.

"You and dozens of others," Ben said. "Why don't you come over and remind me of what you look like in person?"

Ira still lived at home with his parents, in a suburb north of Chicago. His car, a secondhand Mustang that was always breaking down, was in the shop. He borrowed his father's green and white Dodge van and drove to the address in Sandburg Village that Ben had given to him. His heart was pounding as he entered the lobby of the high rise. The doorman asked Ira who he was here to see.

"Roy...Ben Royal," Ira said, almost calling Ben "Roy."

The doorman rang Ben's apartment and then he buzzed the security door and Ira walked through it. Riding up in the elevator, Ira began to feel less nervous and surer of himself. He didn't feel like a suburban teenager anymore. He felt more mature than he ever had before.

His previous sexual experiences had been limited to those with childhood friends and classmates, and the aborted anonymous encounter. Going to Ben's apartment, he felt, was an exciting new chapter in his life. He was entering a new phase, one that was as scary as it was arousing.

Ben met Ira at the door in a silk robe. With the door shut and locked behind them, Ben undressed Ira quickly, leaving his windbreaker, shirt, T-shirt, jeans, white briefs, socks and shoes in the foyer. They proceeded to Ben's bedroom, with a view of Lake Michigan, and had sex for hours. This became their pattern during the year that they saw each other. If they were going out to dinner or a movie or the theater or a party, Ben would insist that Ira arrive at least two hours early so that they could spend some time in bed or in the shower or even on the balcony in a sexual tangle.

Ira was more fascinated with Ben than he was sexually attracted to him. Ben had told him that he was thirty, but Ira suspected that he was older. Ben was an interior designer with an office across the street from the Merchandise

Mart. Most of his clients lived on the Gold Coast, and he was well-respected and successful in his field. Ben also liked to travel, and his apartment was decorated with carvings and sculptures and tapestries and knickknacks from around the globe.

After Ira introduced Ben to Alex and Ruben, two gay friends of his from the theater department at school, they took him aside to tell him that Ben was at least forty, if he was a day. This didn't really bother Ira. His friends weren't saying it because they were jealous. They were more experienced with men. They were just sharing their worldliness with Ira.

Over time, Ira became romantically involved with Alex. He told Ben about it. Ben encouraged him to pursue his feelings, and suggested a three-way, if Alex and Ira were ever interested. After he had his heart broken by Alex, Ira became involved with Ruben. All the while, Ira stayed in touch with Ben, even though they had stopped having sex. Ben seemed to enjoy hearing about Ira's exploits, and Ira liked having someone to tell them to or to ask for advice.

Ira had called Ben on a Sunday morning after a particularly busy Saturday night. It had been a while since they'd seen each other, and Ben invited Ira over for lunch. Both Ben and Ira wanted to see the movie *The Seduction of Joe Tynan*, which was playing at the Village Theater near where Ben lived, so they made it a date. After the movie, Ben asked Ira if he would mind driving him to his friend Todd's apartment. Todd lived on Ashland, just north of Montrose. He was an antiques dealer, and he also sold pot.

When they got to Todd's apartment, he was just about to order a pizza and he asked Ben and Ira if they wanted to have some, too. A pre-season football game, with the sound off, was playing on Todd's TV. Ira hoped that they wouldn't have to watch football while they ate.

Todd turned out to be nice and funny. His mother, with whom he had shared his cluttered six-room apartment, had died a few months before, and Todd was in the process of going through her belongings and taking what he couldn't sell to his clients to resale shops. When Ira told him that he was a theater major at Columbia College, Todd offered to donate what wasn't taken by the resale shops to the theater department to be used for costumes and props.

After finishing the pizza, as Ben and Ira were getting ready to leave, Todd asked if he could come along for the ride back to Ben's. Ira said that would be fine with him. When they dropped Ben off, Todd got into the front seat.

He asked Ira if he would mind dropping him off at Pepper's, a bar he liked to go to in Rogers Park. It was on his way home, so Ira didn't mind at all.

When they got to Pepper's, Todd said, "Come on in. Let me buy you a drink. It's the least I can do since you drove me here."

Ira looked at his watch. It was nine-thirty. He didn't have school the next day, so he accepted Todd's invitation. Ira had never been to this bar before. In fact, most of the bars that he went to, such as the Broadway Limited or Blinkers or Center Stage, were in New Town. This bar wasn't like any of those. It looked very old-fashioned to Ira. The bar itself was made of carved mahogany, and the mirror behind it had a blue tint.

"It's an old art deco bar," Todd said, when he noticed the way that Ira was taking in his surroundings.

"It's cool," Ira said, unsure if that was the correct response.

"Beer?" Todd asked.

"I've got to drive home," Ira said. "How about an orange juice?"

Todd placed the order with the bartender. Ira and Todd made small talk, but Ira could tell that Todd was checking out the other men in the bar. In a way, Ira was relieved. He wasn't really attracted to Todd, and he hoped that Todd's next invitation wasn't going to be back to his place.

The bartender waved to Ira and motioned him over. He put another tall glass of orange juice on the bar.

"This is from the guy with the mustache, playing pinball over there," he said.

Todd came up behind Ira.

"What's going on?"

"Somebody just bought me a drink," Ira said. "What am I supposed to do?"

"Which guy is it? I might know him."

"The dark-haired guy with the mustache playing pinball."

The dark-haired guy with the mustache had stopped playing pinball, and was leaning against the brightly lit machine, facing towards Ira and Todd.

"Oh, I don't know him. Why don't you just lift the glass at him, to acknowledge that you got it?"

Ira did as Todd suggested. The dark-haired guy with the mustache smiled and raised his bottle of beer. Ira could feel his ears getting warm as he locked eyes with the man who had bought him a drink.

"Don't just stand there," Todd said, "go over to him."

Ira walked over to the pinball machine.

"Hi," he said, not sure if the man heard him over the loud disco music.

"Hi, I'm Jason."

Ira and Jason shook hands. Ira's hand was cold from holding the glass of orange juice and from fear. Jason's hand was warm and slightly calloused.

"I've never seen you here before."

"I've never been here before. I'm here with a friend of a friend. I was actually on my way home."

"Where do you live?"

"Just north of here."

"Are you going to tell me your name?"

"Ira. Sorry, it's Ira."

"Do you live alone, Ira?"

"No, I live with my..."

Ira stopped himself before he said parents. He just let the sentence trail off, although he was certain that Jason wouldn't.

"I don't live alone either," Jason said. "I have two cats."

Ira took a long sip of his drink, hoping that Jason would keep talking. He liked the sound of his voice. It was deep and friendly. He thought that he might like it if Jason whispered things into his ear.

"Where do you work?" Jason asked, holding up his end of the conversation.

"I work part-time for my father. He owns a newsstand in the lobby of the Board of Trade building. I'm really a full-time student at Columbia."

"What's your major?"

"I'm a theater major, but I'm thinking of switching to film."

"I love movies," Jason said, and with that, he put his hand on Ira's chest.

"I just saw a movie this afternoon," Ira said, and for a second, couldn't remember the name of it. He was so distracted by Jason's hand.

"I did, too. I saw *The Rose*. Bette Midler was amazing. She should get an Academy Award."

"*The Seduction of Joe Tynan*," Ira blurted.

"What?" Jason asked.

"That's the name of the movie that I saw this afternoon."

"Oh," Jason said. "Maybe tonight we'll see the seduction of Ira."

Then Jason leaned forward and kissed Ira on the mouth. Ira doesn't remember Jason inviting him back to his apartment, but the next thing he knew, he was saying goodbye to Todd and heading for the door.

Jason lived half a block east of the bar. As they walked to his apartment, they talked about the crispness of the evening, about the stars and the moon, about the el train rattling on the rails in the distance.

They were greeted at the door by one of Jason's two cats. The other one was sprawled in the middle of Jason's bed. As they undressed, the cat lifted its head and yawned. Naked, Jason came up behind Ira and gently pushed him, stomach down, onto the bed, almost squishing the cat, who departed in a huff.

The sex was heated and varied. Ira lost track of time. He was too busy keeping track of all the new things he was doing with Jason. The smell of Jason's cologne and Ira's deodorant mingled with the scent of the Vaseline Intensive Care Lotion that Jason used to lubricate both of their dicks and assholes. When the last of their orgasms left them sticky and spent, they lay in each other's arms for a few minutes.

"I have to get up early in the morning," Jason said, the first words spoken that didn't involve sexual directions.

"Do you want me to go?" Ira asked.

"Yes. But I want to see you again. I'll give you my number. Do you promise to call me?"

"Yes," Ira said, as he got dressed.

"I work evenings," Jason said. "I tend bar at Jonathan Livingston Seafood. You can usually reach me in the morning, but not too early."

"I'll call you," Ira said, as he tied his shoes.

Jason walked Ira to the door. He was naked, and his chest-hair was damp with sweat and cum. He kissed Ira good night.

Ira kept his word. He called Jason during the day from a payphone at school, between classes, but there was no answer. If he got home from school before four o'clock, he called Jason, but there was still no answer. It seemed as if Jason was never at home.

A few weeks after Ira met Jason, he took the train into the city to have dinner with some friends from school at the Brewery on Broadway. His car was in the shop again and Ira was seriously considering selling it. A guy named Phillip that Ira knew from his stage make-up class was there. For a while, during the previous semester, Phillip dated a girl named Julia, but they had recently ended their relationship.

While Ira was at the salad bar, putting cucumber slices onto his salad plate, Phillip came up next to him and asked him if he'd done something different with his hair.

"I shaved off my beard," Ira said. "Ruben told me it made me look older."

"That's it," Phillip said. "I like you better without the beard. I feel like I want to kiss you. Would it be okay if I kissed you?"

"Right here at the salad bar?" Ira asked, flattered and flustered.

"Yes, right here."

Ira offered Phillip his cheek, but Phillip landed one right on Ira's mouth. Ira didn't think anyone had noticed, but when they got back to their table, everyone had shifted around so that Ira and Phillip could sit next to each other.

When dinner was over, the group of friends walked to the corner of Belmont and Broadway. Phillip asked Ira to call him, kissed him goodbye, and got on the #36 Broadway bus. Alex and Ruben walked to the Belmont el stop with Ira, chattering away about Phillip and Ira's kiss in the Brewery. Ira hardly said a word. He was more interested in hearing his two ex-boyfriends discuss the event as if it was newsworthy.

Ira looked out the window of the northbound el train as he passed Wrigley Field, Graceland Cemetery, the Uptown Theater, and Loyola University. When he looked out the window at the Morse el station, he saw Jason get off the train with two women. Jason and Ira's eyes met, and Ira thought that he saw recognition flash in Jason's dark eyes. The doors closed and the train pulled away, with Jason and Ira's eyes still locked.

The next stop was the Jarvis station, which was half a block west of Pepper's, the bar in which Ira and Jason had met. Ira decided to get off the train at Jarvis, and go into Pepper's, thinking that maybe Jason would stop in on his way home, especially after seeing Ira sitting on the train.

Since it was a weeknight, the bar was relatively empty. Ira ordered a Coke and reached into his pocket to pay. He pulled out a five-dollar bill and paid for the drink with it. He reached into his other pocket and pulled out two quarters. After paying for the drink, he only had four dollars and fifty cents on him. The train ride home would only cost sixty cents. If he missed the last train going north, he might be able to catch a bus, but he wasn't sure how late they ran. However, four dollars and fifty cents definitely wasn't enough cash to cover the cost of a taxi.

Ira nursed his Coke. There were three other men sitting at the long bar. Two of them were engrossed in a conversation about Chicago politics.

"Jane Byrne is the greatest thing that ever happened to this city," the younger one said. "Who'd have ever thought that Chicago would have a woman as mayor?"

"I don't mind the fact that she's a woman," the older one responded. "I don't even mind that she's the mayor. I just wish she'd choose one of those two things and do it well."

The door to the bar opened and Ira tuned out the political discussion. He looked to see if it was Jason. It wasn't. The man who came in had light brown hair and a thin mustache. He sat down on a bar stool one away from Ira's. He ordered a rum and Coke.

"I see you're drinking the same thing as me," he said to Ira.

"No," Ira said, "it's just a Coke. Trying to keep my wits about me."

"You're in the wrong place for that, isn't he Tony?" the man said to the bartender.

"You're the wittiest one here, Marty," the bartender answered.

Marty turned to Ira.

"Now that you know my name, are you going to tell me yours?" he asked.

"I'm Ira."

"Glad to meet you Ira. You here alone?"

"Yes," Ira said. "But I'm waiting for someone."

"Mr. Right?" Marty asked. "Or Mr. Right Now?"

"His name is Jason. But I don't even know if he's going to show up tonight. I'm just taking a chance."

"What makes you think he'd be here?"

"I met him here a couple of weeks ago. I've been trying to call him, but he's never at the number he gave me."

"He must be pretty special if you're willing to sit here and wait for him."

"I'm not sure how special he is," Ira replied. "It's just that I just saw him when I was on the train before, and I was hoping that he'd recognize me and meet me here."

"Is he a mind-reader? How would he know that you're going to be here?"

"I don't know. But I'm willing to wait for a little while."

"Good luck," Marty said, and with that, he got up and walked over to the jukebox.

Ira began to replay the events of the evening in his head, running them backwards in slow motion. He saw Jason step off the train and onto the platform with two women. He was laughing at something one of the women was saying. As he was walking towards the stairway that led down to the street, Jason looked into the train window where Ira was sitting, and that's when their eyes met. Did Ira smile? Was there something telepathic in his eyes that could transmit recognition to Jason? Did their eyes linger, or did Jason look away quickly? Ira couldn't remember.

Before boarding the train at Belmont, talking under the elevated tracks near the entrance with Alex and Ruben, Ira felt happy and loved. He was glad that he'd stayed friends with both of them, even after their individual romantic involvements ended. Secretly, he still harbored a deep love for Alex, but Alex was too vain and self-involved to realize it. After Phillip unexpectedly kissed Ira in the restaurant, Ira knew that Ruben and Alex would have plenty of gossip fodder for weeks to come.

What should Ira do about Phillip? He'd never given him a second thought. He was handsome and sort of sexy in a corn-fed Midwestern way, but Ira had dismissed him as a straight guy. Ira wasn't interested in seducing straight men with so many gay men available who would be much less of a challenge.

He could hear Phillip's voice in his ear, as if he was standing right next to him. Phillip had said, "I like you better without the beard. I feel like I want to kiss you. Would it be okay if I kissed you?"

Suddenly, it dawned on Ira. Maybe Jason didn't recognize him, because when they'd met, he had a beard. That's got to be it. He was clean-shaven now. When he'd been with Jason, that night, he had a full beard. Ira stood up and looked at his watch. It was midnight. How did it get so late? He dropped a dollar on the bar for a tip and walked outside. He ran down to the Jarvis station entrance, bought a token and ran upstairs to the platform.

He waited about fifteen minutes for the next train to come. While he was waiting, he considered calling Jason from the pay phone on the platform. He'd dialed his number so many times that he'd committed it to memory. But what if he went to sleep as soon as he got home from work? What if he'd gone home with one of those women?

A train arrived and Ira got on and rode it one stop to the end of the line. At Howard station, he tried to find a conductor to ask if there were any more northbound trains to the suburbs. He ran down the stairs to the street level and asked a woman selling tokens in the toll booth, but she told him he had missed both the last train and the last bus.

With three dollars and ninety cents in his pocket, Ira started to walk west on Howard Street, towards home. He walked past the big bank west of the train station and the building on the corner of Howard and Clark that housed both the Pivot Point Beauty School and the Gold Coin Restaurant. Ira hadn't ever been on foot on this stretch of Howard Street. He looked in each storefront window in a cursory fashion as he walked by them. He crossed against the light at Custer and could see the stoplight at Ridge Avenue in the distance. He walked by The Fish Keg and he thought about his father, who liked to get carryout fried shrimp from there. What would his father think of the predicament in which Ira found himself?

When Ira got to the corner of Howard Street and Western Avenue, where the International House of Pancakes was across the street from the Pickle Barrel, he began to feel like he was making progress. That is until he looked at his watch and saw that he'd been walking for more than half an hour and had only gone about a mile. Ira still had at least three miles to go.

He sped up his pace, passing Gulliver's Pizzeria, walking down the stretch of Howard between Western and California Avenues. McCormick Boulevard, where the gothic-looking sanitation system building sat menacingly on the corner, was only a few blocks away. Once Ira crossed the bridge over the Chicago River, he was at another crossroads. Should he proceed west on Howard, down the poorly lit industrial stretch of street, or should he go north on curving and hilly McCormick, where there wasn't a paved sidewalk, and cars often exceeded the forty mile per hour speed limit?

Ira considered taking a coin from his pocket to toss it. Instead, he watched cars zooming by on McCormick and decided that he might be safer on Howard Street. He was standing on the northeast corner waiting for the light to change. As he reached the middle of the wide intersection, the "Do not walk" sign started to flash, and, for a moment, Ira did as it said. It should have been flashing, "Do not leave the house with less than fifty dollars in your pocket" or "Do not sit in a bar and wait for a man who's never home to answer his phone."

A southbound car pulled up to the stoplight and reminded Ira that he needed to keep moving. As he walked alongside the sanitation district's property, the sidewalk ended, and he was forced to walk in the street along the curb. A high chain-link fence surrounded the grounds and when Ira looked through the fence as he passed it, he became aware of movement in the grass. Suddenly, Ira could hear something hitting and rattling the fence from the other side. There were giant rats throwing themselves at the fence and bouncing off it. Ira increased his pace considerably, breaking into a jog. He stopped running when he got to East Prairie Avenue, and walked, panting, to the stoplight at Crawford Avenue.

If he continued walking west on Howard Street, he would eventually have to head north, and his options for doing that were limited. If he took Skokie Boulevard, he would have to walk down the ravine-like S-curve, and after what he'd just been through, he didn't feel like he needed any more obstacles getting in the way of his destination. Ira decided to walk down Crawford instead.

It had never occurred to Ira that somewhere along his route he might run into someone he knew. After all, it was almost two-thirty in the morning on a Tuesday. These were the kind of suburban streets on which it was rare to see someone walking, and not driving, during the day, let alone at this hour.

So, when Scott Goldberg, a former high school classmate of Ira's, who lived with his divorced mother and younger sister, Marla, across the street from Ira's family, pulled up in his shiny black Trans Am near the corner of Kostner Avenue and Main Street, and asked Ira if he needed a ride, Ira just stuttered.

"Ira, man, you're wasted. Get in, buddy. I'll take you home."

Scott opened the door from inside, and Ira got in the car. Wasted, he thought, yes, definitely. Scott knew something about being wasted himself.

A promising career as a track and field star was cut short when he decided to join the burnout crowd behind the high school, smoking cigarettes and pot between and during classes. Ira decided to sit in the passenger seat quietly, acting too out of it to answer any questions. However, that didn't stop Scott from asking them.

"What are you on, man? Pot, acid, Ludes?"

Ira just nodded his head, keeping his eyes glued to his hands in his lap.

"I never pictured you as a druggy, Ira. I always thought you were just one of those theater fags."

Ira lifted his head and glared, blurry-eyed, at Scott.

"Sorry, man, didn't mean any offense."

Scott had always been friendly towards Ira, even though they kept different company, which is why Ira was surprised at his remark. Ira needed to think of a way to repay Scott's kindness.

Scott turned onto their street, and as luck would have it, found a parking space right in front of Ira's house. He turned off the ignition.

"We're home, man. You'd better be careful going inside. Don't want to wake up the parents. You're in no condition to explain."

Ira once again lifted his head from a lowered position and looked at Scott with what he hoped was gratitude and love. He leaned over and kissed him, square on the mouth.

"Thanks for the ride," Ira said, and got out of Scott's car, happy to finally be home.

DEFENDING KAREN CARPENTER

In the basement of Robby and Ricky's parents' two-flat, one floor below their widowed grandma's apartment. After we'd finished our daily rehearsals to all-boy garage-staged shows, where we'd lip-synch and pretend to strum guitars and run our fingers across keyboards that weren't plugged into electric outlets (in much the same way The Partridge Family did), we'd huddle together, not touching like football players did (although I would have if someone had asked). We opened our flies to expose ourselves and compare our individual and collective growth of a less obvious nature.

I often thought about Karen Carpenter. How she wouldn't have passed judgment on us. How she wouldn't have screamed and yelled at us, the way Robby and Ricky's grandma did that time when we didn't hear her sneak up on us from behind.

At the onset of puberty, I found myself expending an awful lot of energy in defense of Karen Carpenter. With my voice cracking, and my legs still weak from the growing pains of the night before (pain so great, I imagined myself riding to Crawford Junior High School on the school-bus-yellow Dodge van with the disabled kids and playing wheelchair basketball in gym class), I was vocal in my opposition to anyone who dared to put down the dark-haired angel from Downey.

It was like when Davy, the sexy, skinny, scary older guy who lived across the alley from Robby and Ricky with his creepy sisters and even creepier parents would invite us over and give us things just for the chance to run his sexy, skinny, scary fingers over our rapidly metamorphosing bodies. Davy was the adult who supplied me, the bookish one, with contraband copies of *The Exorcist* and *The Godfather*, two books that instilled a fear of Catholicism in me, a fear greater than that of the devil, the mafia or child molesters. Karen would have understood the small price I paid for knowledge and experience, a gnawing quest as persistent and bottomless as appetite.

I believe it was Karen Carpenter who saved me from thinking about how the white-blonde hair I was born with darkened a quarter of a shade with every birthday; my only distinguishing mark in a family of mousy-haired dullards taken away without my permission. How my younger brother continued to pummel me into submission in front of his friends as well as my own. I would listen to Karen complain beautifully about "Rainy Days & Mondays," while I rubbed the aching, just punched parts of my arms, chest and stomach, and know that if anyone could save me from the cruelty of the world, it was Karen Carpenter.

And when I began to deprive myself of food, part contest, part punishment, it was Karen's dulcet tones that harmonized with the singing from my shrinking belly. I believe it was Karen Carpenter who, without much fanfare, died for my, for all our sins.

BEST FRIEND

Joseph Schoenmeister had a wandering eye, a tracheotomy scar, grayish skin and buck teeth. He had a cowlick and a nervous tremor. I sat next to him at lunch, that first day of sixth grade, in a new school. It only seemed natural since we ended up sitting next to each other in homeroom, language arts and social studies. He was in a more advanced math class and I was in a more advanced science class.

Joseph loved milk and bought three of those little square cartons. I was allergic to milk and felt myself gagging when he sucked every drop out of all three cartons through a skinny white straw.

It was nice to have someone to feel like an outsider with. Joseph had gym class in the morning. Mr. Bruce, the gym teacher gave all the sixth graders a tour of the locker room and showers, more of the new territory that came with being at Lincoln Junior High School. He wheeled out the gym class mannequin wearing the navy-blue gym shorts and gold t-shirt that were the school's uniform colors. Mr. Bruce slid one of the legs of the shorts up to reveal one of the leg-bands of the jockstrap we would all be required to wear under our uniforms during gym the next day and every day after that for as long as we were in school.

"And then what?" I asked, between bites of my salami sandwich.

"And then he made us go into the gym, take off our shoes, choose teams and play dodgeball until the bell rang. When do you have gym?"

"After social studies, which is after lunch."

"I have science after lunch," Joseph said. "Luckily we don't do dissections until seventh grade, because I don't think I could stomach it."

"So," I said, wanting, but dreading, to talk more about gym class. "You picked teams..."

"Yeah, being one of the new kids, I had the advantage. Neither team wanted me. I would have been just as happy sitting this one out, but Mr. Bruce put me on the skins team."

"Skins?" I asked.

"You know, shirts versus skins. So, we took off our shirts and had balls thrown at us. By the time three o'clock rolls around, the welts should be gone."

"Did you have to shower?"

"No," he said with a look of undisguised relief, "the key to the storeroom where the towels were kept was lost. Besides, nobody has locks for their lockers yet. Tomorrow, it's the showers."

And just as he said that Michael Lieberman walked by.

"What was that?" he said to Joseph, kind of leaning on him.

"Leave him alone, Lieberman, he wasn't talking to you."

Lieberman ignored me and applied pressure to the elbow he had in Joseph's back. Joseph looked at me in confusion, his good eye wide as a veal calf's.

"I just want to ask my girlfriend a few questions," Lieberman said to me. "Aren't you in my homeroom?" he asked Joseph.

"Yes," Joseph said, his voice sounding calmer than he looked.

"I forgot your name. What is it again?"

"Joseph," Joseph said.

I gripped the sides of my lunch tray, rubbing both thumbs along the fiberglass edges. I wanted to lift it over my head and start banging it on the Formica tabletop. I wanted everyone to stop eating and pay attention. Lieberman was getting away with it again.

"That's right, now I remember Miss Barry calling your name. She asked if you would rather be called Joe or Joey, and you said Joseph. Joseph Shoemaker..."

"Schoenmeister," Joseph said, his face losing its grey and going magenta.

"Achtung, Schoenmeister," Lieberman said, "I am Herr Lieberman."

And then Lieberman smacked Joseph in the back of the head.

"That was for nothing," he said, and as he started to walk away, "next time I'll have a reason."

Joseph and I walked towards our lockers in silence. As luck and the alphabet would have it, our lockers were directly across the hall from each other. What could I tell him about Michael Lieberman that he didn't already know? Only that the firepower of Lieberman was nothing in comparison to what happened when he joined forces with his accomplice, the notorious class clown, Jonah Katz.

Jonah Katz left me alone. We had been friends in elementary school. We went to the same Hebrew school, after school, three days a week. If his antics were wildly hilarious during the day, they took on an even more maniacal twist in the late afternoon and early evening. I didn't want to be included in his schemes; dropping pencils near the desks of girls in mini-skirts, hiding the chalk and erasers, which sent the Israeli teacher into a cartoon-like fury, locking the boy who knew the Hebrew alphabet by heart in the coat closet.

All the other kids at Hebrew school thought Jonah was the funniest thing since *Laugh-In*. That's because they all went to Old Orchard Junior High. By late in the day, Jonah's pranks became stale. I'd seen them all before. Earlier in the day at Lincoln Junior High, the year before at Madison School, in Little League. He didn't want to alienate me, maybe because he thought I could be of some use along the way. I stayed quiet.

Because of Jonah, Michael Lieberman left me alone. I was still taunted during gym, but that was to be expected. Because of Jonah, the focus was usually shifted away from me and onto some other equally undeserving target. But I had a reputation that fall that I was afraid I would never shake.

At the beginning of sixth grade, I didn't have a best friend. In fact, I hadn't had a best friend since the summer before fifth grade, when I stood by helpless and watched my then best friend, Danny Gold, get beat up by Johnny and Jimmy Miller, the terror twins from St. Peter's School. I would have helped him, but their younger sister Janice, wearing her plaid jumper and knee socks, was holding me in an arm lock from which I couldn't break loose. When they'd finished with Danny, they took turns knocking me around a bit, but I got off easy. They'd broken Danny's glasses, given him a black eye, a bloody nose, a split lip and bruised the rest of him pretty good.

"A girl is stronger than you are," Danny said, disgusted at the revelation and spitting blood. That was the last thing he ever said to me.

When word got around that summer, I knew that fifth grade would be almost unbearable. As it was, I had already been pegged as something of a weakling and a coward. I preferred to think of myself as a pacifist and an intellectual. Wasn't there enough fighting going on in the world, I would argue just as the first punch was being thrown my way. Aren't we learning anything from Vietnam? I would ask as I struggled to catch my breath after having the wind knocked out of me. Apparently, the answer was no as the punches kept coming and I thought of Martin Luther King, Jr., the Kennedys and Gandhi.

The little war between the kids who attended the public schools, most of whom were Jewish, and the ones who went to Catholic school raged on without a cease-fire in sight. Danny Gold, who was never given a second thought by Michael Lieberman and his kind, was suddenly thrust into the spotlight as celebrity martyr. He was first choice when teams were picked in gym class, he sat at the most crowded and popular table in the cafeteria at lunch and he was being invited to more parties than he could attend.

As time went on, he became more forgiving, occasionally seeing fit to nod at me or even say hello if we crossed paths in school or saw each other at a movie, in a store, or at the library. But he changed in a way I'd never expected. Danny altered his shape like mercury and soon mirrored the actions of Michael and Jonah. He spent less time at the library and more time at the park and the bowling alley. Even his greetings towards me, that had been slow in returning, subsided. We were running in different packs.

Joseph Schoenmeister was an "accident," the youngest of four by eighteen years. He had a niece who was one year older than he was, which fascinated me. Joseph's parents were a few years younger than my own grandparents, and there had been talk in his family of Joseph's father's impending retirement.

Joseph and his parents had moved to Skokie from Indianapolis the summer before sixth grade began. Mr. Schoenmeister had owned a party-goods store in downtown Indianapolis. His store had been robbed twice in one year, once while he was closing and once overnight, when no one was around. Joseph's older sister Johanna, who had moved to Skokie with her husband, a dentist, a few years before impressed upon her father the fact that there were no stores in the area that sold all the necessary decorations for a child's birthday party. There were lots of young couples with little children in town. She sent them the real estate section from the local neighborhood paper, circling the ad for a vacant storefront across the street from the bakery, in downtown Skokie, that would be a perfect location for a party goods store. Mr. and Mrs. Schoenmeister agreed, and the wheels were set in motion.

Joseph and I were having lunch in the restaurant on the top floor of Montgomery Wards after a morning of shopping. He was telling me the story of his family's relocation. Things moved very quickly, he said. He remembered one day finding himself standing in the middle of the living room in the house on Carson Way, surrounded by empty boxes.

His parents explained that they were moving to Chicago so that they could all be closer to his sister and her family. Since James, the brother closest to Joseph's age, had died in Cambodia, his parents seemed to do things without much planning or purpose. Joseph liked the school he went to in Greenwood. He had friends whose houses he liked to play at after school and on weekends. Joseph's mother gave private piano lessons in the family parlor. His friends' parents were very understanding about having Joseph play at their houses more than their children played at his.

Mr. and Mrs. Schoenmeister bought a two-bedroom house on Brown Street in Skokie, one block from the new store. As the date of the grand opening approached, Mr. and Mrs. Schoenmeister asked Joseph if he wanted to help them think of a new name for the store since the old store in Indianapolis had been named for the street on which it was located. He had been distant from them since the move, and they wanted to include him in this project. They wanted to feel like a family again.

"Why don't you call it 'Party Headquarters'?" he said and then went into his room and closed the door.

There were more girls than boys in Miss Barry's homeroom, but at my end of the alphabet, there were more boys. So, as it happened, I had Joseph Schoenmeister to my left and Michael Lieberman to my right. Michael's best friend, Jonah Katz sat to Michael's right. Jonah knew all of Jerry Lewis' movies by heart and was working on committing to memory every episode of *The Honeymooners*, which was being rerun on channel 32 every weeknight after the news. Jerry Lewis was his God, but Jackie Gleason was his Son of God. He would say, Two of the greatest comedians of all time's names begin with J and I am going to be the third. The way he said it, everyone believed him, even Miss Barry.

Show and Tell was something only little kids did. We were in junior high now, on our way to bigger and better things. Instead of Show and Tell, we had Shared Interests Time. Twice a week, half an hour before the bell rang signaling the end of the day, homeroom turned into a circus of hobbies and talents. Collectors and singers, collagists and drummers were given ten minutes each to display some hidden gift to the rest of the homeroom.

Jonah Katz had a nickname for almost everything and everyone. He referred to Shared Interests Time as ShIT. If there had been something of particular interest to him, he would say, The ShIT really hit the fan today. Or if it was boring, he would say, sniffing the air, I think someone stepped in ShIT. Jonah shared his humor with us.

He would do imitations of Mr. Black and Mr. Howard, two of the other sixth grade teachers. They were middle-aged men who shared an apartment in the city. They were more than an item of curiosity for me. Even though I wasn't in either's classes, I constantly made a point of saying hello to them in the halls, in the lunchroom, anywhere they were within my line of sight. I was fascinated by them and only slightly obsessed.

Jonah Katz would also imitate Lily, the woman who was in charge of the cafeteria. Depending on his mood, he would change before our eyes into a miniature Don Rickles and start attacking one of us. Miss Barry had to intervene, cutting him off before his time was up.

I loved music and would usually bring in the latest forty-fives or albums that I'd bought. Joseph and I had that in common. We both loved The Beatles, Barbra Streisand, and The Carpenters. After school, if neither of us had too much homework, we would walk over to the Record Shack and flip through the bins. We had differences in opinion, too. He liked Blood, Sweat and Tears and I liked Chicago.

We both secretly liked *The Partridge Family* and each swore never to betray the other. Once, we even went as far as to admit that we both thought David Cassidy was cute. I went too far, though, when I told Joseph that I thought he was cuter than Bobby Sherman. He looked uncomfortable with that revelation, so I never brought it up again.

Joseph lived closer to school than I did. I usually rode the school-bus home. Sometimes, I would walk home with him and, if his mother didn't have a piano student, go inside for an after-school snack. This didn't happen very often since I had Hebrew school on Tuesdays and Thursdays, but when it did, we had a good time. Joseph usually came to my house on Saturdays. We would take the bus, or my mother would drive us to the movies or the malls at Old Orchard or Golf Mill.

One Saturday, Joseph came with my parents and me when we went to the store my father's sister, Aunt Simone, owned on Devon Avenue. It felt funny going to Aunt Simone's store, which specialized in greeting cards and invitations for special occasions, when Joseph's father had a store that sold pretty much the same thing. We were going to pick out the invitations for my Bar Mitzvah, which was a little over a year away.

"Why don't we get the invitations at Party Headquarters?" I had asked at dinner the night before.

"Because they only sell invitations for baptisms and first communions," my mother said, although I was sure she had never been in the store.

"Besides," my father said, "we promised Aunt Simone that we would give her our business. She is family, after all."

"Can Joseph come with us tomorrow?" I asked.

"It won't be very interesting for him," my mother said. "Once you've been in one card store, they're all pretty much the same."

"I don't think he's ever been to Devon Avenue," I offered. "I don't think he's even been to Kiddieland."

"Probably not," my mother said, and then looking across the table at my father, "well, okay."

After dinner, I put the dishes in the dishwasher and then I called Joseph.

"Ask your Mom if you can go shopping with my parents and me tomorrow. We're going into the city to get some stuff for my Bar Mitzvah."

"Your what?" he asked.

"My Bar Mitzvah," I said. "That's why I go to Hebrew school three days a week."

I realized then that he'd never asked me about Hebrew school. My mother once said that there probably weren't any Jewish people in the town where Joseph grew up and that living in Skokie would be a culturally enriching experience for him. I found it hard to believe that he'd never met anyone Jewish. In Skokie, I knew people who were Catholic, Protestant, Lutheran, Methodist, Christian Scientists and Seventh Day Adventists. My mother said it was because we lived in such proximity to a large metropolitan area.

"When I turn thirteen," I told Joseph, "I'm going to have a Bar Mitzvah. It means I will have become a man."

Saying that felt funny. I was short for my age, shorter than Joseph. My voice hadn't even begun to crack like some of the other boys at school.

"There will be something at the synagogue and then a party after that with family and friends. I'm going to invite you to it."

"Will they let me in to the synagogue?" he asked.

"Why wouldn't they?"

"I'm not Jewish," he said, sounding uncertain. "Do I have to convert?"

"No," I said, "you don't have to be Jewish to go to a Bar Mitzvah. Now, ask your mom about tomorrow."

Joseph put his hand over the mouthpiece, and I could hear their muffled conversation.

"Thanks, Mom," he said to her after uncovering the receiver, and then to me, "she said it was all right."

"Good," I said, "I'll call you before we leave the house. Talk to you tomorrow."

I felt lucky to have a friend like Joseph. Even though we came from such different backgrounds, we laughed at the same things and liked to read the same kinds of books. We were both in the chorus at school and talked often about careers in show business. Joseph wanted to be in plays, and I wanted to make movies. We tried out for the spring Talent Show in a play we wrote ourselves, but our names were not on the list when Miss Nunn put it up on the bulletin board outside the auditorium.

At the bottom of the piece of paper it said that Miss Nunn was still looking for people to be on the stage crew. Joseph and I thought that that would be a good way to be a part of things and volunteered our services.

Michael Lieberman and Jonah Katz were in the talent show. They were going to do a scene from *The Honeymooners*. When I congratulated Jonah in homeroom, he offered to autograph my forehead. On the first day of rehearsals, the cast and crew wandered around the auditorium, jumping on and off the stage and banging on the piano.

Miss Nunn came in and brought things to order in her quiet, Southern way. She asked me to oversee the lights and Joseph to be in charge of the props.

The rehearsals went well and sometimes ran late, past five. My mother would pick me up at school and offer Joseph a ride. He usually declined, preferring to walk home alone, feeling good about being involved in such an exciting theatrical endeavor. A couple of times, my mother let me miss Hebrew school as the date for the Talent Show got closer.

One day, Joseph was absent from school with the flu. It was a week before the Talent Show, and I knew which props belonged in which scenes from watching the rehearsals while operating the lights. Miss Nunn agreed to let me help until Joseph returned. I went backstage to organize the props. Michael Lieberman and Jonah Katz were talking to Sandy Goodman. Sandy was going to sing "As Long as He Needs Me" in the Talent Show, accompanied by her best friend Ellen Abber on piano.

"Hey, where's the Nazi?" Lieberman asked.

"I don't know what you're talking about," I said, afraid that I did know.

"Herr Schoenmeister, the little Hitler," he said, walking towards me. He stopped a few inches from me, clicked his heels and raised his arm in a Nazi salute.

"You know," he said, "Jews aren't supposed to be friends with Nazis."

"Joseph isn't a Nazi," I said.

"Schoenmeister is a German name, isn't it?" Jonah said.

"Yes, but..."

"But what? Nazis were German, so that makes him a Nazi."

"That's right," Lieberman said, "and his father probably ordered the murders of my grandparents and aunts and uncles. His father probably made sure my parents were put into a concentration camp. But he didn't count on them getting out and coming to America."

"Joseph's father wasn't even born in Germany," I said, not sure if that was true. He was a very tall man with grey hair and bloodshot eyes. He never said much, and I wasn't sure if he spoke with an accent or not.

"He is a Nazi," Jonah insisted. "And we know he has secret Nazi meetings in the backroom of his store."

"How do you know that?" I asked, not sure whether to believe them, a little afraid of being presented with the truth.

"He thinks he has everyone fooled, but not us. The name of the store was the dead give-away. 'Party Headquarters'!"

"What are you, stupid or something?" I asked and started to laugh.

Then Lieberman grabbed me by the ear. I had to bend forward a little as we walked back towards where Jonah was sitting with Sandy.

"Who's stupid now?" Jonah asked.

Lieberman squeezed and began to twist my ear. I could feel my eyes sting with tears. Sandy giggled and covered her mouth.

"We're going to teach your friend a lesson," Jonah said. "We're going to rewrite history."

"We?" I asked, certain that he didn't mean me too.

"We," he mimicked, "you and me and Lieberman."

"I don't want to teach anybody anything."

Lieberman jerked my head up by the ear, jarring a tear loose from my eye, which slid across my nose and dangled from my chin.

"You don't have any choice in the matter. Unless you'd like us to personally deliver you to the Miller doorstep. It seems they still have some unfinished business with you."

I pictured a bully network, underground and sinister, where victims were delivered by hand in dark basements and abandoned parking lots, regardless of loyalties. Lieberman released me and I wiped at the tears with the backs of my hands. I just stared at Jonah through blurry eyes.

"That's better," he said, "now here's the plan..."

At that exact moment, Miss Nunn poked her head through the door leading to backstage.

"Rehearsal is about to begin. Everyone in their places."

That night, I called Joseph to see if he was feeling any better. He told me he would be back in school the next day. He asked me about rehearsal, and I told him it went pretty well, that Maria Rotini was getting closer to having the Sylvia Plath poem she was performing committed to memory. I wanted to tell him about the threats that Katz and Lieberman had made, but I didn't know how.

"Well, see you tomorrow," he said.

"See you tomorrow," I said, and then we hung up.

As the night of the Talent Show got closer, the cast and crew took on a more serious attitude. There was less clowning around during the dress

117

rehearsals. After one act finished performing, everyone watching in the auditorium, waiting in the wings and doing tech work would cheer with unbridled enthusiasm. We all knew that our parents and friends would be proud of our entertaining efforts. The tap-dancing sisters, Donna and Dawn Nelson, were in synch. Sandy and Ellen were in tune. The gymnasts were in shape. Jonah and Michael were in rare form. And I feared the time when they would do what they had only threatened.

The evening before the Talent Show, a Thursday, Joseph and I stopped into Albert's Place, the store that sold black-light posters and printed t-shirts, next door to the movie theater. There was this flickering lightbulb mounted on top of a 7-Up can that I'd been saving my allowance to buy. Joseph was walking through the maze of black-light posters, oohing and aahing, while I was trying to decide between a red or blue flickering bulb. I saw Jonah and Michael walk by the store's window and hoped that they didn't see me. A few seconds passed and then they were looking in the window again.

I looked away from the window, down at the glass counter, at the array of flavored rolling papers and bongs. I heard the bell above the door ring as they came into the store and walked up behind me.

"Get the Zig-Zag," Lieberman said, "my brother says it burns better."

"I'm not buying papers," I said.

Jonah walked towards the black-light poster maze and I heard the hanging wooden beads at the entrance clicking as he entered it.

"Hey, Lieberman," he said, "look who's here."

Joseph came quickly out of the maze's exit with Jonah hot on his heels. He looked at me and then over to the door.

"I can't decide right now," I said to the hippie salesman behind the counter. "I'll be back tomorrow."

"What's the hurry?" Jonah asked.

"No hurry," I said, "I just think I'd make a better decision tomorrow."

"You know, you can buy a black-light bulb and screw it in on top, too," the hippie salesman said. "We sell the black-light bulbs in a couple of different sizes."

"I'll be back tomorrow," I said, and then, "You ready to go, Joseph?"

He answered by walking to the door. I followed him, with Jonah and Michael behind me. We walked past the Skokie Theater, Joseph and me walking next to each other, with Jonah and Michael a few paces behind. *Love Story* was playing. Joseph and I had seen it the Saturday before. We both cried and tried hard not to let the other one see.

"'Love means never having to say you're sorry'," Jonah read aloud from the poster.

"No but killing six million Jews does. Isn't that right, Herr Schoenmeister?"

"I don't know what you're talking about," Joseph said as we both started to walk faster.

"Just ignore them," I said to Joseph, "don't make them mad."

"I haven't done anything to them," Joseph said, "why should they be mad?"

As I was about to answer, I felt a hand on my shoulder. Before I knew what was happening, Jonah and Michael had wedged themselves between Joseph and me. We walked this way, four across, past the Coach and Four Restaurant, across Oakton Street, past Desiree Restaurant, the drug store and then they guided us into the gravel driveway next to Canton Chinese Restaurant.

It was the end of rush-hour in downtown Skokie. People were hurrying to get home on foot or by car. It was easy to miss something in the flurry of activity. If anyone had been paying attention, this is what they would have seen.

Jonah pinned me against a wall and breathed a threat of pain in my face if I moved or made a sound. Michael took Joseph's books and notebooks away from him, then bent over a little, as if he was going to place them on the ground. Then he dropped them. He pushed his chest up against Joseph's. They were practically the same height, their eyes glued to each other's saying different things. Everyone's breathing sounded different; Jonah's like laughter, mine like choking, Lieberman's like some kind of wild animal's, Joseph's like an old man's.

"Do you pray?" Lieberman asked Joseph.

Joseph didn't answer. He seemed to be looking at me out of the corner of his eye, until I realized his bad eye had wandered.

"He asked you if you prayed," Jonah said.

"Answer him," I said, "then maybe he'll leave you alone."

"Yes," Joseph said in a voice that surprised us all.

"Show me how you pray," Lieberman said.

Joseph turned his head and looked directly at me with both eyes. What was that look? Fear? Hatred? Love? I'd never seen it before from anyone. I felt my shoulders shake, as if I were crying, but nothing came out. To Joseph, it must have looked like I was laughing. He looked away from me. His knees cracked as he bent them and knelt.

"What about your hands?" Jonah asked.

Joseph must have been trying hard not to let his hands shake while he brought them up in front of him, the palms meeting, because they twitched spasmodically, like a heartbeat.

"I'll bet you're praying that we don't kill you," Lieberman said. "I'm going to tell you what you should pray for. Forgiveness."

"Forgiveness, for what?" Joseph asked, his voice losing its control. "I haven't done anything."

"For being a Nazi," Lieberman said. "For killing six million Jews."

"I didn't kill anybody," Joseph said.

"Ve haff been vatching you," Jonah said, doing his best German accent. It was a cross between Arte Johnson on *Laugh-In* and Colonel Klink on *Hogan's Heroes*. I had had enough.

"Get up, Joseph," I said, starting to walk away from the wall, "we don't have to take this from them."

Jonah put his hands on Joseph's shoulders to keep him down. Lieberman came at me, his hands in fists before him.

"I should kill you, too," he said, his voice like a grown-up's, deep and swollen with anger. "Doesn't it bother you to be seen with him? Don't you know what his family did to my family?"

"You don't know what you're talking about," I yelled back at him, "you don't have any proof."

"I have all the proof I need," he said. "Proof that he's a German Nazi and that you're a traitor."

He opened one of his fists and slapped me across the face. I started to raise my hand to the hot spot on my face, but let it drop in a defeated fist to my side. Lieberman picked up Joseph's social studies book.

"It's all in here," he said, raising the book over his head and bringing it down on top of Joseph's.

Joseph's body seemed to crumple from the blow. Jonah put his hands under Joseph's armpits, pulling him back up to his knees. He put his hand under Joseph's chin, which for a moment, appeared to be a gesture of kindness. Joseph's eyes were closed, and I wasn't sure if he was unconscious or if he had closed them in anticipation of what would come next. This time the book came at him from the side, like Lieberman's slap across my face. His head was turned in my direction and this time I closed my eyes. I heard the book dropping onto the white gravel driveway. I opened my eyes and Jonah and Michael were gone.

"Joseph," I said, "Joseph, can you hear me?"

Joseph stood up very quickly, I thought, for someone who'd just been through a beating like that. His right cheek was dark and swollen, a bruise already insinuating itself. He steadied himself against the brick wall as he bent over to pick up his books and notebooks. He left the social studies book where it was. I bent over and picked it up, held it out to him, but he ignored it.

We walked to the end of the driveway, across the alley and through the old fire station's paved driveway. As we got closer to his house, I wanted to say something to him. What would he say if I told him that I'd known that Jonah and Lieberman had been planning this? That I didn't know whether to believe them? That my instincts were wrong? That the bad guys didn't always wear black pants, white shirts and ties, and blazers from Catholic schools? That sometimes, when a person thinks they are going to right a wrong, they never think they may be wrong, too? That I was trying to be the best friend I could be, for whatever it was worth.

When we got to the sidewalk in front of Joseph's house, I still hadn't figured out what to say to him. Aside from shame, I felt an overpowering love for him that was more than brotherly. I had underestimated him. He was so much braver than I.

He turned right and walked up the sidewalk to his front door, not looking behind him to see if I was there. I started to call his name, the social studies book in my outstretched hand. If I were him, I probably wouldn't want to see *Our World of Wonder* for a few days either, if ever again. I did what any best friend would have done and took it home with me.

"See you tomorrow," I called after him as he closed the big front door.

I started to walk away, when I heard the front door open, the brass door knocker banging.

"See you tomorrow," he said, waving, looking suddenly like an old man, instead of the naive boy that he was. And I knew I would see him, and others like us, for so many tomorrows to come.

THE INDISCRETIONS OF A POET

Max and Shane had been dating seriously for about three months when Shane's ex Tom called.

"I still love you," Tom said, "I don't think I can live without you."

"I'm sorry," Shane said, "you must have the wrong number."

Shane hung up the phone as if it had been on fire. He walked back into the bedroom in the house that he shared with Felice and Dorrie in Cleveland Park. Max was lying in the bed, naked except for the top sheet which covered his calves and feet. One of the three pillows was against the wall at the top of the bed and he was leaning against it, with his hands behind his head. The other two pillows were on the floor. Shane reached for the bowl of water on the nightstand that had a washcloth soaking in it. He wrung the washcloth out and began to wipe the rivulets of semen off Max's stomach and chest.

"Why do I still want to smear this stuff all over my face and lick it from my fingers?"

"Because you know you're not supposed to," Shane said. "We always want to do things we're not supposed to do. Like answer phones after sex."

"I thought you left the answering machine on."

"Dorrie or Felice must have turned it off. One of them must be expecting a call."

"Then why didn't one of them answer it?"

123

"I'll have to ask them," Shane said, and leaned over to kiss Max. End of discussion.

When Shane first considered accepting the position of poet-in-residence at St. Denise's All-Girls Academy in Washington, D.C., Tom was very enthusiastic.

"I think it will be really good for our relationship," Tom said. "We've never really had any physical distance between us and besides it's just for a year."

It sounded convincing. Shane had just finished doing a two-year residency at a small, private technical school in Boston, where Tom worked as a lawyer at a prestigious law firm. They had met in 1984 at a party, thrown by a mutual friend, right after Shane moved to Boston from Evanston, Illinois, where he'd grown up and attended college. They fell into a heated and fast-moving romance and Shane moved into Tom's penthouse apartment at Longfellow Place. Luckily, Shane found someone to sublet the dark, cramped Beacon Hill studio apartment he had just signed a one-year lease on the week before.

Tom was a few years older than Shane and, as Shane thought, more worldly wise. He'd had his first male lover when he was still in high school and they stayed together until their sophomore year of college. Shane had spent most of high school writing love poems to boys on the wrestling, gymnastic and basketball teams and hiding them in a safety deposit box in a bank.

In college, Shane had a gay poetry professor who was married to a lesbian art history teacher and women's archery team coach. Dr. Horsham opened Shane's eyes to a world that he'd been too sheltered to believe existed. Horsham introduced him to the works of Allen Ginsburg and Walt Whitman, Paul Verlaine and Oscar Wilde. Shane was so relieved to find the poetry by these men. All sorts of possibilities presented themselves.

One afternoon, after class, Dr. Horsham and Shane rode their bicycles over to the bank where he kept his poems in a safe deposit box. They sat by the fountain, in front of the bank, and Horsham read them, all two hundred and fifty-nine of them. Some of the poems were just a few lines long; others were a few pages. He kept tisking and grunting while he read them. Shane had heard him make similar sounds in the classroom, when a student read something they'd written, that he liked.

"How do you feel about publishing?" he asked.

Shane didn't know what to say. He'd never thought about publishing those poems. They were kind of personal, and Shane said that to him.

"Personal," he repeated, "and universal at the same time. You just might be the voice of a new generation. Do you have any others?"

Lately, Shane had begun to write about the guys who played frisbee in a park near the college. It was the spring semester of his junior year. The weather was beginning to get warmer and the frisbee players often played shirtless, in cut-off jean shorts. He wrote about them leaving the ground to catch the whirling, fluorescent-colored, plastic disks and taking flight. Hovering above the giggling co-eds who were grounded and awestruck.

"Yes," Shane said, and that's how it all began.

Dr. Horsham introduced Shane to an editor at a publishing house interested in experimental poetry. The man's name was Monty Austin and he came to their first meeting with a contract in hand.

"Roger Horsham spoke highly of your work. He even sent me some samples and I must say I was very impressed. You have a strong sense of voice and the line. From what I've seen, you are extremely prolific. How would you feel about two books of poems being published simultaneously?"

Shane was speechless. He had told his parents at dinner the night before that he was meeting with a publisher the next day and they were as visibly excited as a tax lawyer and a registered nurse could get. Shane's younger sister was the only one who seemed to be enthusiastic. She had just discovered Sylvia Plath and Anne Sexton and was genuinely excited about having a poet in the family.

"If you self-destruct," she asked, "will you leave me your record collection?"

Shane quickly changed the subject, realizing he was on his own.

Locker Room Confidential and *Teen Meat* were released at Christmastime that year. Both books were well received by the press. Shane was reviewed in the book sections of all the major newspapers across the country. The phone at his parents' house was so busy, they had to have a second, private line installed.

Having two books of poetry on the best-seller's list was a strange way to tell your parents that you are gay, but that's just how it happened.

At first, they were disappointed for the wrong reasons. They had thought that Shane was stashing away money in that safe deposit box. So, in a way, they were relieved that he didn't have a cache of money that was made by selling stolen goods or dealing drugs to high school kids. But they still had their reservations.

"Gay, huh," his father said to no one in particular. "You don't wear your mother's clothes in the house when there's no one around do you?"

"No, Dad," Shane said, trying to sound as reassuring as possible under the circumstances.

"You don't hate women do you?" his mother asked, sounding a bit hurt and responsible.

"Not at all," he said and gave her what he thought was a reassuring kiss on the cheek.

"You gotta boyfriend?" his kid sister asked.

"Not at the moment," he said.

And that made him think and wonder if this sudden popularity would bring on a flood of romance where there had only been drought.

Shane was never any good at accepting a compliment. His friend, J.J., threw a party for him when the books went into their second printing. Shane had also just graduated and was mulling over what to do with his future. There were almost as many people in attendance at the party that he knew as there were those he didn't. During the course of the party at J.J.'s loft in Printer's Row, he was introduced to so many people that he began to call them by the wrong names. When an old friend arrived, someone that he'd grown up with and went to high school with, he had to stop and close his eyes for a second before saying hello, because he couldn't remember his name.

"The fame is going to your head," he said and walked away, momentarily insulted.

Shane followed him to a table where an androgynous-looking man poured drinks.

"Scotty, I'm really sorry. I think I've met more people tonight than I ever met my whole life."

"Apology accepted. At least you're still humble."

"How did you get here?" Shane asked.

"I drove," Scotty said, "You want to leave?"

"Yeah," he said, "I'm going to say goodbye and thank you to the host."

"I'll be in the car. It's parked across the street."

Scotty and Shane went for a long drive that night, talking and reminiscing about the old days. Scotty was managing the men's department of one of the older downtown department stores. Shane decided to bounce an idea off of him.

"There was a girl at the party tonight who goes to school in Washington," I said.

"State or D.C.?"

"D.C. She told me that the poet-in-residence is leaving at the end of the term and that they are looking for someone to replace him."

"Are you going to apply for the position?"

"I'm thinking about it," Shane said. "I also met a guy who runs a private school in Boston who is looking for a poet-in-residence, too."

"Why don't you apply for both?"

"What if I get both jobs?"

"Take one and see about doing the other later on. We both know that your popularity is going to last. At least, I know that. This is not a fluke."

"Thanks," Shane said, not sure if he agreed with Scotty's assessment of him. The next day, he applied for both jobs.

The administrators at St. Denise's were very understanding when Shane told them that he'd accepted the poet-in-residence position at the Boston American School. He told them that he'd signed a two-year contract and if there was ever an opening at St. Denise's in the future that he'd like to be considered for it.

Shane left for Boston in early summer and had no trouble finding an apartment. A girl he went to high school with was enrolled at Harvard, and he called her when he got to Boston. She invited him to a party at her house in Central Square.

"This will be a good opportunity for you to meet new people," Rebecca said.

"I'm not much of a party person," he said.

"Come anyway," she said, "it's just a small get together."

There must have been two hundred people milling about in the four-bedroom apartment Rebecca shared with seven other women. Near the front door was a table stacked with copies of his books.

"I work at the Harvard Book Store," she said by way of explanation. "I thought that while you were here, you might sign a few copies, maybe treat us to a reading."

"Rebecca, if I had known that this is what you had planned, I never would have...."

"I know, you never would have come. But here you are. And looking awfully cute, too."

Rebecca slipped an arm through his and cleared her throat loud enough to get the attention of the revelers.

"The guest of honor has arrived. He has consented to give us an impromptu reading of his work."

Shane ended up reading about half the poems in each book. The party guests were extremely receptive and enthusiastic. His mouth was so dry when he finished reading that he drank two glasses of club soda.

"What do you look like without any clothes on?" a tall man with short brown hair asked.

Shane had the last mouthful of soda in his mouth and almost choked.

"Arnold Schwarzenegger?"

"Maybe a before photo of Arnold Schwarzenegger," Shane said after quickly gulping down the drink.

"What do I have to do to find out?" he said.

"Well, you can start by telling me your name."

"If I tell you my name, will you sign my book?"

"If you tell me your name and where you live, I'll sign both books."

That's how he was introduced to Tom. They quietly slipped out the back door of Rebecca's shared apartment and hailed a cab on Massachusetts Avenue. Tom grabbed a hold of one of Shane's nipples through his shirt and gently moved his thumb and index finger back and forth while staring into his eyes, until they pulled into the driveway at Longfellow Place. Tom only let go when he had to reach into his pocket to pay the cab driver.

They had rough and tender sex until the sun rose a few hours later. Tom got out of bed and put the jockstrap he'd been wearing back on. As Shane drifted into sleep, he heard him say, "I'll be back."

He woke up later that afternoon to find Tom looking at him from a chair in the corner of the room.

"What floor are we on?" he asked.

"The top," Tom said. "Are you hungry?"

"A little," he said. "Where's the bathroom?"

"In there," and Tom pointed to a door across the room.

In the bathroom, Shane looked at himself in the mirror. He said his name to himself, recited his new address and phone number. He just wanted to make sure that he hadn't completely lost his mind. When he came out of the bathroom, Tom was in the bed waiting for him. He was looking at a carry-out menu.

"How do you feel about Chinese?" he asked.

"That's fine," Shane said.

"Will you stay?" he asked, and he did.

The two years flew by faster than Shane had expected. He and Tom became well-known as a couple in Boston's literary scene. Tom came to every reading he did and, when he had the time, helped him plan some of his lectures at the school. It was a very productive and positive period for both of them. At the same time, he began to feel Tom growing away from him.

The contract with the Boston American School had ended, and ironically, the position at St. Denise's had become available again. Shane applied for the job but was torn between staying in Boston with Tom and leaving for Washington. His third book, *Safety Pin*, had just been accepted for publication and he was making plans to go to New York for a reading.

"I'm going to sit this one out," Tom said, "if you don't mind."

"Not at all," Shane said, minding it very much.

He had begun to rely on Tom's presence at the readings as a stabilizing influence. He felt like he had been pushed out of a nest before he fully understood the concept of flight. This was as good a time as any to learn.

The New York trip was a big success, but he was missing Tom. He decided to return to Boston one day earlier than scheduled. When he got to their apartment, there were two young, blonde sailors going at it in their bed, while Tom sat in his chair in his corner of the room and watched.

Until that time, Shane had vacillated about going to Washington to become poet-in-residence at St. Denise's. He had been giving serious thought to staying in Boston, finding another teaching position. Tom was overly apologetic. He was lonely, he'd said. It made Shane wonder how many other poets and sailors he'd picked up during their relationship. He decided to accept St. Denise's offer. Tom begged him to stay in Boston. Shane told him that he didn't think it was a very good idea. That was when he said that thing about Shane's leaving being a "really good thing for their relationship."

What relationship? he wanted to ask.

He didn't know anyone in Washington, D.C. Marcella, Shane's agent, put him in touch with Bob, a friend of hers who ran a bookstore and coffee-house in DuPont Circle. They had dinner together a few times, but soon discovered that books and coffee were the only things they had in common. The only thing, that is, until he met Bob's roommate.

They were having dinner at The Childe Harold, shouting at each other so that they could be heard over the music and conversation of the other diners. Bob kept looking at his watch, like he had somewhere important to rush off to after dinner. Shane began to rely on his lip-reading ability instead of trying to hear what Bob was saying. He was mouthing something about a book signing that he had organized for the following week, when he stopped talking, stood up and waved vigorously towards the front door.

"There's someone I want you to meet," he said.

Shane stood up, too, and turned around. He saw a man who was about his height, with medium length black hair and the greenest eyes he'd ever seen at a distance coming toward them.

"Max," Bob shouted in a voice Shane didn't know he'd possessed, "I want you to meet Shane Albert."

Max extended a hand big enough for both of Shane's and they shook.

"Shane Albert," Bob repeated in the same booming voice, "the poet."

There were two women, probably in their late thirties or early forties, eating heaping salads at the table next to theirs. They were looking at the three of them standing around their small table for two, shouting introductions and shaking hands.

"Excuse me," the one with the grey streaks in her hair said, "but I was wondering if you would mind..."

"I'm sorry," Shane said, "I'll get the waitress and see if she can bring another chair."

"Oh, that's okay," she said, "I was just wondering if you would sign my copy of *Tiger Meat*?"

She pulled a beat-up copy of the book out of her bag and handed him a ballpoint pen with teeth marks all over it.

"My name is Adrian," she said.

After he finished signing her book, the waitress arrived with a third chair, having noticed the commotion they were causing.

"Would you mind signing this cocktail napkin?" she asked Shane pushing the chair in under Max.

They stayed at the table for another two hours. Max played in a band called Horseshoe Prince. He gave private music lessons during the day, while the other band members waited tables or worked at Commander Salamander or Tower Records.

Max and Bob invited Shane back to their apartment on Columbia Road, but he was suddenly very tired. They seemed like such a happy couple, it only reminded him of how lonely he was.

The next morning, the phone rang as Shane was getting ready to leave the house for his first day of classes at St. Denise's. His housemate Felice knocked on his bedroom door.

"You have a phone call," she said, "someone named Bob."

There was a phone on a small table in the hallway outside of their bedrooms. Shane missed the telephone man on the day that he was supposed to install his private line in his room and hadn't had a chance to reschedule a new installation date.

"Hi, Bob. What's up?"

"Max really liked you. Is it okay if I give him your number?"

"Why would he want my number?" he asked. "I thought he was your lover."

"Oh, no," Bob said as if offended, "we're just roommates."

"Just roommates," Shane repeated, trying to remember what Max looked like.

He had tried not to be too obvious while he memorized every detail about him, because he thought he and Bob were an item. Wavy black hair and green eyes with little flecks of yellow. He had dimples in both cheeks and a strong chin. He was clean shaven. He wore a diamond in his left ear.

"Give him my number," he said, "I'm home most nights after six."

Max picked Shane up at home, the evening of their first date. They were living in the enlightened age of safe sex, and he had bought a box of condoms that afternoon at a drug store across the street from St. Denise's. While he wasn't sure of the direction that their night was going to take, he wanted to be prepared.

Felice and Dorrie were sitting in the living room, watching an "Odd Couple" rerun when he came downstairs.

"Here's Shane," Dorrie said in the voice of a fashion show runway announcer. "He's wearing an over-sized white cotton shirt, a black leather bolo with a sterling silver and genuine turquoise clasp. Black Levi's and black cowboy boots. Looks like he's ready for a night on the town."

"You look like Dwight Yoakam," Felice said, "Where's your ten-gallon hat?"

"Cut it out," Dorrie said, "I think he looks nice."

"Planning on doing a little roping and tying tonight?"

"Do you think I should wear something else?" he asked more than a little self-consciously.

"Don't listen to her," Dorrie said, "the only roping and tying she ever gets to do is to her tomato plants in the garden."

"I'm really nervous," he said. "I feel so out of touch. I think that Tom may have ruined me for other men."

"I was only kidding," Felice said. "You look smashing."

Outside, they could hear an emergency brake being clicked into place and a car door open and close.

"Is it okay if we stay here?" Dorrie asked. "Would you mind introducing us?"

"Not at all," he said, and then there was a knock on the door. Introductions were made, and he gave Max a brief tour of the house.

"We have reservations at Lauriol Plaza," Max said, "we really should be going. It was nice meeting you both."

"Same here," they said in unison.

Dinner was wonderful. They talked about growing up, how they both ended up in Washington. About writing and music and art. They talked about success and failure. After dinner, they walked into DuPont Circle and sat on a bench near the fountain where skinheads skateboarded and shot fierce looks at anyone who looked at them too long.

Max drove him home and walked him to his door and kissed him good night. It was a slow and musical kiss and he was excited by the prospect of the neighbors watching. It was Monday night and they made a date for Friday night. Max said he'd call Shane the next day.

The first floor of the house was deserted. He walked into the kitchen and got a can of Tab from the refrigerator. When he got to the top of the stairs on the second floor, both Dorrie and Felice opened the doors to their respective rooms and they sat on the floor in the small hallway and talked about love for hours.

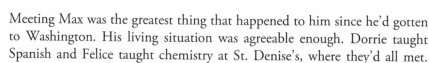

Meeting Max was the greatest thing that happened to him since he'd gotten to Washington. His living situation was agreeable enough. Dorrie taught Spanish and Felice taught chemistry at St. Denise's, where they'd all met. They'd been sharing the house for about six years before Shane moved in.

He enjoyed teaching creative writing to his students, but his life had begun to feel incomplete. His relationship with Tom was such a big part of his life in Boston that being alone in Washington was more of an adjustment than he'd been prepared for. At the point of desperation, he had begun to read the personals in the *Washington Gay Weekly*, but that only depressed him more.

Max filled a void in his life and provided love and affection in abundance. He was becoming consumed by the relationship, but in a good way. He maintained his newly discovered independence while carrying on a romance. Most of all, being with Max helped him forget about Tom.

The first time Tom called during this period took Shane totally by surprise. They had talked on the phone a few times after he'd moved to D.C., but he no longer had feelings of any kind for Tom. He'd stopped loving him, hating him, thinking about him.

So that Sunday when he called, Shane was completely thrown for a loop. Was he drunk? Was he horny? Was he crazy? If Tom called again, he'd have to tell him about Max. That it was really over between them. But he didn't call again. Instead, he sent a letter. It arrived on Tuesday and was followed by two more on Wednesday and two more on Thursday. The letter on Friday contained photos of them from Tom's photo album. The pictures were from one of their many trips to New York. Standing in front of the Statue of Liberty, ice skating at Rockefeller Center.

He was looking at the pictures on a Saturday afternoon when the phone rang. He was expecting a call from Max with details of the plans for that night.

"So, what's the scoop," Shane said when he answered the phone.

"That all depends on your preference," Tom said, "vanilla or chocolate."

"Tom?" Shane said, his voice a mixture of disbelief and fear.

"Do you want a sundae or a cone?" he asked, still playing the game.

"I'm sorry, I was expecting someone else."

"Oh yeah, what's his name?"

"Max," Shane said, defiantly.

"Max," Tom said, mockingly.

Shane took a deep breath and a moment of silence hovered between them. Tom broke it with a sigh.

"You have no idea how much I miss you," he said.

"You have a funny way of showing it," Shane said. "Why are you calling? Why are you writing me letters? I have a new life here and it doesn't include you."

"I want to be a part of your life again," he said, sounding desperate.

"You had your chance," Shane said.

"I want to see you," he said. "I'm coming to town."

"Please don't. I don't want to see you. You'll be wasting your money."

"I'm coming to town on business," Tom said, "the firm is opening an office in D.C. and they're sending me down to help set up the litigation department. I'll be there all of next week."

"I can't see you," Shane said, "I'm seeing someone else."

"Just for dinner. My treat. Just to talk. Just to see you."

"No," he said, hoping that he sounded like he meant it. "I have to go."

"Please," he said as Shane hung up the phone.

He turned on the answering machine and let Dorrie and Felice know that he was screening his calls. The phone rang a few minutes later and he stood over it, waiting for the answering machine to click on after the second ring. The message began, "You have reached the residence of Shane, Dorrie and Felice. Please leave a message and go in peace."

Max's voice came over the little speaker.

"It's Max. I'll pick you up..."

Shane turned off the answering machine and lifted the receiver to his ear.

"We've been getting obscene phone calls, so we're just screening them now," he said, trying to sound believable.

"If that keeps up, you should think about getting a new number." Max's concern was too much.

"We will," Shane said.

"I'll see you at 7:30," Max said, "bring an overnight bag."

During the creative writing course Shane was teaching, Alice appeared in the doorway. She was the secretary to Mrs. Green, the dean of students.

"You have a visitor. He's waiting outside of Mrs. Green's office."

Shane excused himself from his students and followed her down the hall.

"We don't usually allow guests during class time, but he was very persistent."

"I'm sorry," he said, "I'll see that it doesn't happen again."

Tom was sitting in the little alcove outside of Mrs. Green's office. The door to her office was open and he could see her sitting at her desk, peering at them over the tops of her half-glasses. They went outside to talk.

"You could have gotten me into a lot of trouble. I told you I didn't want to see you and I have my reasons."

One of the reasons became immediately apparent the moment Shane saw him. He was still so incredibly sexy to him. Suddenly, all the bad things seemed to turn into smoke and disperse before his eyes. They never really had a proper break-up and there were so many things that were still left unsaid. Shane wondered if he agreed to go to dinner with Tom if he would have the chance to say them.

Shane spoke, "I'll have dinner with you tonight. Just dinner. We can talk and say goodbye."

"I'm staying at the Willard. We can have dinner at the restaurant in the hotel. How's seven o'clock?"

"Fine," Shane said, "I'll see you there."

"Let me pick you up," he said, "I rented a car."

Shane thought for a second. If he picked him up that would mean that he'd have to come to the house. He wasn't so sure that he liked that idea.

"I bought a map," he said, "I found your street on the map."

He sounded so pathetic. Shane gave in.

"Just honk," he said, "I'll come right out."

As he had suspected, dinner was an emotional amusement park. One minute they were on the Tilt-A-Whirl, angrily spinning and being thrown into each other, then they were heading into the Tunnel of Love. The Merry-Go-Round turned into a roller coaster. Shane could sense the Haunted House was just around the corner and he was running out of "E" tickets.

Tom said he hadn't been with another man since Shane left. He told Shane that he hadn't washed his pillowcase, after he'd left, for six months, because it still smelled like him. At one point he began to cry softly, and Shane could feel tears welling up in his eyes, too.

Was he really cold and heartless? Just because he was looking out for his own best interests. Tom had hurt Shane terribly. But he was still his first great love. And now, he was in love with Max. He told this to Tom.

"Oh, please," he said, "spare me the details. You don't love him. He was just there to catch you on the rebound."

"You're wrong," Shane said, "I was over you when I met him."

"That's what you think," he said. "I saw that look in your eyes when you saw me today, sitting outside of Dean Green's office."

"Mrs. Green," Shane said, correcting him. And he knew he was right. He hadn't wanted to see him because he knew it would just stir up old, unresolved feelings. he was trying very hard to repress those emotions.

"I have a new life here," Shane said, "one that doesn't include you."

"You said that already. I also know that you have a new lover. We have a history."

"We had a history," he countered.

"Shane, I'm asking for another chance."

"I'm not so sure that you deserve one."

"Let me try and make it up to you. We belong together. Boston hasn't been the same since you left. And neither have I."

They finished dinner shortly after that and Tom drove him home. Shane couldn't speak. He was more confused than he'd ever been. His fourth book,

Valley of the Guys and Dolls, was set to be released in a few days and that was on his mind. It was just too much to think about. They pulled up to Shane's house on shady, tree-lined Woodley Road.

Shane thought about inviting Tom in but changed his mind. He leaned over to give him a good-night kiss on the cheek and their mouths met. Pretty soon, they had their arms around each other and were rubbing and stroking. Tom moved his hands to the button on Shane's pants and opened them. He buried his face in Shane's crotch. They were double-parked and Tom had his emergency flashers on. He grabbed Shane's erection and moved his hand up and down. Tom sucked one of his balls into his mouth. Shane put his hands on top of his head. His mouth felt familiar and right. He could hear a car pulling up behind them.

"You have to stop," Shane said, "we have to stop."

Tom looked up at him and there were tears in his eyes, again.

Quickly fixing his clothes, he said, "Call me when you get back to the hotel," and got out of the car.

There were two messages on the answering machine from Max. Shane dialed his number as he got undressed. His clothes smelled like Tom's expensive cologne and he wanted them off.

"How was school?" he asked, catching Shane unprepared.

"How come you didn't say hello?"

"Well, I knew it was going to be you calling. Call it a seventh sense."

Bob, Max's roommate, had joked about a seventh sense. He said it was something that developed between two people involved in a new and serious relationship. It was more powerful than any of the other senses, including the mysterious sixth.

"School was fine," Shane said, trying to remember how it was. The whole day seemed foggy now.

"We got a gig at the Burning Flag, two weeks from Saturday. We just found out about it today. Mark it on your calendar. I'll get you a backstage pass."

Max, and the other members of Horseshoe Prince had been trying to get booked into the Burning Flag for a while. It was a popular new club located between DuPont Circle and Georgetown. The booking meant that they had finally met one of their goals.

"That's wonderful," Shane said, "congratulations."

"I couldn't wait to tell you. That's why I called twice."

"I'm sorry I wasn't here to get the good news sooner. I was out with some of the teachers."

He couldn't believe how easy it had been for him to lie to Max. He didn't even hesitate. Immediately, he felt guilty and sorry for having lied.

"I'm really tired," he said, "long day."

"I won't keep you," Max said, "I just wanted to say good-night. And I love you."

"I love you, too," he said, feeling like a liar and a sneak, even though he meant it.

When he woke up the next morning, the light on the answering machine was blinking. The message was from Tom. He must have slept through his call. Tom wanted to get together for dinner, again. He suggested having room service in his room. He said that he was leaving the next day and it would be their last chance to see each other, face to face, for a while.

Shane called his hotel and left a message at the desk saying that he wasn't available for dinner. Then he called Max.

"Can I spend the night?" he asked.

"Sure," Max said, "but we'll have to go to sleep early. It is a school night after all."

When they hung up, he packed a bag to take with him to school. He left a note for Dorrie and Felice, letting them know that under no circumstance were they to give out his whereabouts for that night. He would explain everything to them when he got back the next day.

All day at school, he dreaded the appearance of Alice in the doorway of his classroom with the announcement that he had a visitor. But he worried for nothing. His classes went well, and the day moved at a good pace. After school, he caught the Massachusetts Avenue bus to DuPont Circle and transferred at Connecticut Avenue. He got off the bus at Florida Avenue and walked the few blocks to Max and Bob's. It was a warmer than usual November and most of the people on the street were wearing shorts and t-shirts. He took off his blazer, loosened his tie and unbuttoned the top two buttons of his shirt.

At the entrance to the apartment building, he crossed paths with a young girl whose hair was dyed a dark eggplant color. She was carrying a guitar case decorated with peace sign decals. He imagined her to be one of Max's guitar students. He could see him, leaning over her, helping her with finger placement on the frets. Max had an enormous amount of patience and they had even talked about him teaching Shane to play guitar, even though they both agreed that he was tone-deaf.

Shane rang the bell and Max buzzed him in without asking who it was through the intercom. He was standing in the hall when Shane got to the top of the stairs. The door to the apartment was wide open and he could hear "Avalon" by Roxy Music playing. Max took his briefcase and his jacket. Once inside the apartment, he took Shane in his arms and they kissed. Shane dropped his other bag where they were standing, and Max lifted him up. He wrapped his legs around Max's waist. Max carried Shane into the bedroom, leaving a trail of shoes and clothes as they went.

Naked, on his stomach, Shane tore open a condom wrapper and handed Max the condom as he knelt behind him massaging and gently probing his ass with his hands and fingers. Shane imagined him playing him like his guitar, with great concentration and affection. He heard him squeeze the tube of KY-Jelly and felt the cold lube on his fingers as he slid them into him. Shane pushed back into his hand, gripping the sheets. In an instant, his fingers were out and his sheathed penis was in. Shane winced and relaxed, taking it all. Max wrapped his arms around him, circling his nipples with his fingers, still moist from the lube. He moved one hand down between Shane's legs, while he pushed himself up, against him more, with both arms.

Later, while they were in the shower, they heard the front door open and they knew Bob was home. He knocked on the bathroom door.

"Master Max," he said in his best butler's voice, "where would you like Master Shane's belongings."

"In my room, if you don't mind, Jeeves. We'll be dining out tonight."

"Very well, sir," Bob said. "Will that be all."

"Yes, Jeeves, you are dismissed."

"Well, fuck you very much, sir."

"You're very fucking welcome, Jeeves."

Bob declined the invitation to join them for dinner. He said that he was meeting some friends for a drink at JR's and asked them to stop by after dinner.

Max and Shane got one of the tables by the window at the Odeon Cafe. Sissy, the only woman band member in Horseshoe Prince, was their waitress. She pulled a chair up to the table and sat with them while taking their orders.

"Tuesday must be Guppies night out," Sissy said, motioning with a sweeping gesture towards the restaurant filled with gay yuppies.

"At least they're big tippers," Max said.

"Oh, darlin', don't get me wrong. I'm not complaining. It's just nice to think that some of these adorable guys are looking at me for me and not wondering if they can fit into this skirt or these pumps."

"Don't worry about us," Max teased, "we just want your blouse."

"Oh, you," she said and got up to take their order to the kitchen.

It was then that Shane saw Tom, standing in the entrance to the restaurant. He was with another man and a woman. They were laughing, trying to move out of the way of two men on their way out. Shane looked down at the table, at his hands in his lap.

"What's wrong?" Max asked, sensing a change in him.

"Nothing," he said and half-smiled, his head still half-bowed.

"You look like you've just seen a ghost."

Shane shook his head, not lifting it.

"Are you okay? Do you want to leave?"

"No," he said, nodding his head.

"I'm not sure what that means. Please look up, at me."

"I can't," he said. "Something's wrong with my neck."

"You want me to rub it for you?"

"No. Please. It'll be all right. I'll be all right."

Just as he said that, he saw a familiar pair of Gucci loafers approach the table.

"Shane? Is that you?"

It was Tom. He'd left his dinner companions and come to the table alone.

"Yes," Shane said, his head still down.

"I waited for you to return my call, but you never did. So, I made other plans," he looked at Max. "I see you did, too."

Shane didn't like the sound of his voice and he could just imagine the way that he was looking at Max. Shane lifted his head and looked at Max.

"Max, this is Tom, my ex-lover from Boston. Tom, this is Max, my lover."

Max started to stand, to shake Tom's hand.

"There's no need to get up," Tom said, "I can already see that you're a big, strong boy. Don't let me interrupt your dinner."

Tom started to turn away and then stopped and turned back.

"Oh, by the way," he said. "I bought you a plane ticket, if you want to come visit me in Boston. If you're not doing anything two weeks from Saturday. I thought we could spend your birthday together."

He pulled the ticket envelope out of his pocket and left it on the table.

"Bon appetit," he said and, this time, walked away.

Max looked at Shane, a little stunned.

"I can explain," he said, not really sure if he could.

Max didn't say anything for a few moments and then got up from the table.

"I need some air," he said and walked out of the restaurant.

Shane took his napkin out of his lap and put it on the table as Sissy was approaching with their drinks.

"Where you going, darlin'? Where's Max?"

"I'm sorry, Sissy. We have to leave. Wrap our orders up and I'll come back to get them."

"Wait, darlin'," Sissy yelled as Shane was on his way out the door. "You forgot this."

She was holding up the airline ticket. Shane hesitated. She brought it to him and he went to look for Max outside. He looked up the street, in the direction he would be heading to go home, but he couldn't see him. He looked in the direction of the Circle, but Max wasn't anywhere to be seen. He walked for a few blocks, first in one direction and then the other. He thought about going to Max's apartment, but wasn't sure if he would let him in. He hailed a taxi and went home.

For two days, he left messages on Max's answering machine. Bob wasn't even picking up the phone. He tried calling Bob at the store. He was so cold, that Shane imagined icicles forming on the telephone lines.

"Well, this ought to give you plenty of material for your next book of poems."

"Bob," he pleaded, "don't you want to hear my side of the story?"

"No, and neither does Max. You really hurt him. Do you have any idea how important that show at the Burning Flag is to him? He really wanted you to be there. But you can't. You're going to Boston for the weekend. Well, I hope it's a memorable trip. And a memorable birthday."

"Let me explain," Shane said.

"Don't bother," Bob said and hung up.

Since they started seeing each other, Max had been an endless source of inspiration. Shane had begun a series of sonnets, a form he'd always found too restrictive, about Max. Writing about him had given him a new appreciation for rhyme and iambic pentameter. When Shane thought about him, he heard music. Not just because he was a musician, but because he reminded him of an enduring love song. Honest and romantic and sincere.

Shane typed up one of the sonnets and signed his name to it. He bought a card and put the poem inside. He went to a florist in Adams Morgan and ordered him a dozen roses and gave specific instructions that the card be sent with the flowers.

Thursday night was when the band usually met at Max and Bob's before going to their rehearsal space across the street. Shane called, hoping Max would answer and he did.

"We're on our way out the door," he said.

"Please," Shane said, "just give me a minute."

There was silence on his end, which he took as a sign that Max was listening.

"I wanted to tell you about Tom sooner. I thought that I could handle him myself. When he wants something, he goes after it with a vengeance."

"Was he the `wrong number'? The `obscene phone caller'?"

"Yes," Shane said.

"Why didn't you tell me? I would have helped. Did you ever tell him about us?"

"Yes," he said. "But he didn't care."

"Do you care?" Max asked.

"Very much," Shane said. "Did you get the flowers?"

"Yes," he said, "and the sonnet."

"I meant what I said."

"I know. I just need a little time away. I need to think things out. We were moving very quickly. Faster than I'd realized. Now, I'm not sure if I'm ready."

"I am," Shane said. "I'll wait if you want, if you need time."

"Yes," was all Max said.

"I'll let you go," he said.

"Before we hang up," Max said, "are you going to be in town for the show."

"Yes," he said.

"Good. I'll leave a ticket for you at the box office."

Max hung up without saying goodbye.

Shane went to that concert. Horseshoe Prince played better than he'd ever heard them play before. He didn't get to go backstage as he'd hoped. Rumor had it that there was a talent scout from a major record label there that night. Max and Shane hadn't talked since that last phone call. But he'd kept his promise and left Shane a ticket to the show.

Shane put the airline ticket to Boston in an envelope and mailed it back to Tom. Tom hadn't called him either. The letters stopped coming. Shane wondered what his motives had been. Was it a momentary lapse, or had he meant the things that he'd said?

Shane was sitting alone, on his birthday, in a crowded and smoky club. Horseshoe Prince finished playing their first set and the audience members were milling about, refreshing drinks, standing on line at the bathrooms, talking all at once.

Under Shane's arm, he had a large manilla envelope that he'd meant to mail before arriving at the club, but he couldn't find a mailbox. Inside was the manuscript for his next book of poems. His agent was expecting it, but she'd have to wait until he was ready to send it. Shane was having a little trouble coming up with a title. He was thinking about calling it *Discretion Advised*.

MY MOTHER'S VANITY

There was a mascara smear on one of the monogrammed pink hand towels. It was in the shape of a child's primitive rendering of a tree, leafless in autumn. You might think, "That's a lot of mascara," and it was.

What made it worse was that I denied having anything to do with it. Novice liar. Who else could have done it? Did I think my mother was that oblivious? She always made sure to wipe the peach lipstick streaks from the mouthpiece after she hung up the white princess phone. I was the one who regularly forgot to do the same.

I'll say this. I knew enough to stay out of her closet, away from her clothes. The bras and panties and girdles and garters, the stockings and tights, the negligees and nightgowns from Schwartz's Intimate Apparel held no interest. Neither did culottes, see-through and opaque blouses in silk, rayon and cotton, colorful pantsuits and jumpsuits, clam diggers, mini, midi or maxi skirts, dresses, plaid or striped slacks, jumpers, cashmere and angora sweaters, pastel shells, or patterned shifts, corduroy and denim blazers.

Sure, I might slip a bare foot into a stiletto heel, a pump or strappy sandal. She had small feet; we were practically the same size. I avoided the zip-up wet-look boots in white, black, fire-engine red and sky blue. I worried about stuck zippers. I didn't want to get into something I couldn't get out of quickly.

But how could I avoid her vanity? The tortoiseshell comb, the matching onyx hairbrush and hand mirror, the hair clips and pins, the clip-on bows and velvet headbands. My thick, pitch- black hair a shimmering reflection of her regularly dyed coif; dark and resilient as black lacquer.

Was it my artistic streak that led me to swirl fingers, brushes and other applicators in the powdery terrains of rouge, blush and eye shadow? Imagine the eyelid as a canvas. A blank slate beckoning for color and contrast. Eyebrow pencils in their own murky hues. Cool and damp eyeliner, outlining and emphasizing.

Lipstick tubes containing vaguely phallic rockets of tint and shade, iridescent and ethereal or bright and flushed. The waxy warmth caressing and coloring lips, accentuating kisses, puckers, smiles and frowns. Every lip-printed tissue was stashed and trashed.

No wonder they call the device used to apply mascara a wand. It contains magical powers, transforming lashes that are too short, too light, too limp, too wispy into sculpture. Even the shyest eyes command attention when lashes are darkened and dramatically drawn out, like living picture frames. The sensation of dipping the bristles into the tube and gently dragging the brush along the fine hairs is electrically charged.

Next came the masking of the faintly chemical smell of the palette's potions. So many pretty bottles in such distinctive shapes; Tigress and Woodhue by Fabergé, Jean Naté, Estée, Topaz by Avon, Halston and Jovan's Musk Oil. Pulse points. So little goes such a long way.

Her jewelry box had a similar effect. How else to complete the process? Bangles and beads, costume jewelry and clip-on earrings. Gemstones and rhinestones. Pearls and plastic geometric shapes. Cocktail rings and chokers. Gold and silver-plated baubles. Multi-colored bubble watches for wrists. Chains and strands, and timepieces worn as necklaces.

Did I feel cute? Desirable? Seductive? Glamorous? New each time? Indestructible? Older than my single digit age? You bet I did.

That time that the handsome bearded guy at the indoor flea market told me I was pretty enough to be a girl; my father went ashen. I didn't even have a lick of make-up on my face. Maybe I didn't need it after all. Maybe I just needed to stand still and be adored for my natural beauty, something on which neither my mother nor father could agree. I was the perfect blend of their facial features, skin tones, hair texture; all in miniature. They always looked at me as if they couldn't decide if that worked in my favor or theirs.

One day I got careless, sloppy, reckless. One day was all it took. For someone so good at making sure that compacts clicked shut silently, that glass bottles never clinked, that lipstick points never dulled, that eyebrow pencils stayed sharpened and the shavings were properly disposed of, that no speck of powder, no matter how pale, was left behind, I really blew it.

Cold cream was involved. Soap and water, too. Foam and scrubbing. Something stinging in my eye. More warm water. The burning sensation subsided, although the blurred vision persisted. Reaching for something terry-cloth soft to dry and comfort. Something left behind.

I was watching television or reading a book. I was drawing a picture of a face, not mine, or coloring in one in a coloring book. I was making paper snowflakes or construction paper links. I was building something with Lego blocks or playing with Matchbox cars when my mother called me into the bathroom and pointed to the monogrammed hand towel, now monogrammed with something else.

I lied. I denied. I whined. I cried. I ranted. I recanted. I stomped my feet. I folded my arms. Tears fell. Snot bubbled and dripped from my nose. It tasted like perjury.

What else could I do on that day but destroy the evidence? Piles of Maybelline, Cover Girl, Max Factor, Revlon, Helena Rubinstein and Yardley products heaped in the center of my parents' king-size bed. Every bottle of perfume poured out as an accelerant. The offending towel ignited by my father's butane lighter and dropped where it could do the most damage. I would use the ashes like kohl to enhance my eyes, my best feature, blinking and blazing as the house burned down around me.

WHEN JESUS CAME BACK
TO SKOKIE

Don't you remember? It was early October 1997, at the beginning of the High Holy Days. Jesus sat towards the back of the #97 Old Orchard bus, smiling to Himself at the numerical coincidence. He tried His best to be inconspicuous. Reluctant about making eye contact with the Polish and Latina maids, on their way to work, who would surely recognize His familiar profile quicker than those Russian Jews or godless teenagers clutching skateboards.

He gripped the bright yellow Sports Walkman that he bought on closeout at Howard Street Electronics before boarding the bus. Only He knew that in a few years, the device would become obsolete, just like 5 ¼ inch floppy discs, Earth Shoes, payphones, and Republicans.

He listened to the Amy Grant tape the African-American salesclerk had insisted on giving to Him because, as the kid said, He looks so much like a young Richard Gere. He took notes in a journal with a rendering of the Mighty Morphin Power Rangers on the cover using a No. 2 pencil He made with His bare hands.

As the bus headed west on Howard Street, He recalled that the south side of the street was Chicago, and the north side of the street was Evanston. Without touching them, He opened the windows on both sides of where He sat, just a crack, so He could take in the sounds and smells. Children laughing and running on the sidewalk. The scent of fried fish and chicken from JJ Fish and baking pizza from Edwardo's.

149

He thought gasoline prices were high as the bus passed a filling station at the corner of Howard and Ridge. How strange it was to see Bethesda Hospital, just west of Western Avenue, sitting vacant after all these years, considering all the sickness and death on earth.

It genuinely moved Him when the bus-driver stopped to pick up a man in a wheelchair at the corner of Oakton and Dodge, how the other passengers swiftly vacated the seats that flipped back and folded up to make room for the differently-abled man. Privately, He marveled at the hydraulics of the vehicle, the way the front end of the bus lowered, like a camel, so that the man could roll easily aboard.

At Oakton and McCormick, as the bus crossed out of Evanston and into Skokie, He noticed a decided difference in the air pressure. It was as if all the women on their way to cleaning houses had drawn in one collective breath of dread and refused to let it out. Suffocation being preferable to servitude.

Having listened to both sides of the Amy Grant cassette, He pressed the stop button on the Sports Walkman. Before taking out the tape and slipping it into its case, He read the little booklet containing the liner notes and the lyrics, some of which caused Him to blush. The bus crossed Crawford Avenue. He averted his eyes at the sight of the Jews For Jesus storefront, appalled at the contradiction in terms.

Jesus really expected to see tumbleweeds blowing through the deserted, ghost-town streets of downtown Skokie. He was more than a little relieved to see the brick and stained-glass majesty of St. Peter's church, where Lincoln Avenue and Niles Center Road split.

This was where He hung out in August 1969, the first time he visited the purported "Village of Vision." Blending in with the other hippies with long hair, beards and sandals, wandering the summer streets. Congregating near the intersection of Oakton Street and Lincoln Avenue, in front of Desiree Restaurant.

Almost everyone had transistor radios pressed to their ears or dangling from straps around their wrists. According to the 5th Dimension, it was "The Age of Aquarius," and Jesus was swept up in the fervor of the fantasy. He especially enjoyed singing along with Dusty Springfield's "Son of a Preacher Man."

Everyday people of all ages clustered in the doorway of Little Al's Record Shop, on Oakton, just east of Niles Avenue. They were snapping up 45s of "Galveston" by Glen Campbell, "Sugar Sugar" by The Archies, "Crimson and Clover" by Tommy James and the Shondells, "Hair" by The Cowsills and "Jean" by Oliver. He almost stopped a little blonde-haired boy from buying "In the Year 2525" by Zager & Evans, but he didn't want to burst the kid's bubble.

A little more than 2,000 miles away, another man with a beard and long hair, claiming to be a different kind of messiah with a dedicated coterie of devotees, was committing a crime as heinous as crucifixion. If He could have, Jesus would have flown like Superman through the sky to 10050 Cielo Drive in Benedict Canyon. He would have spoken in His most soothing, yet authoritative voice, explaining how what they were doing was wrong and cruel, evil and unnecessary.

But Jesus found himself distracted by the giant, illuminated, red blown-glass piece of fruit that hung, as a shingle, in front of the Apple women's boutique. Young women in dirty and frayed bell-bottom jeans entered, alone or arm-in-arm with their boyfriends and left carrying shopping bags overflowing with chic mini-skirts and frocks, patterned and see-through blouses, and other groovy fashion finds of the era.

To this day, Jesus alternates between feelings of guilt and powerlessness about not being able to be at two places at once despite what others might think or have been led to believe. He feels a big fat tear roll down his cheek, like the one shed by the Native American man in the 1971 "Keep America Beautiful" PSA TV commercial.

On down the road, at the corner of Niles Center Road and Greenleaf Street, He smiles to Himself to think He couldn't have better planned the placement of the Carson's Ribs restaurant directly across the street from the Temple Judea reformed congregation.

Suddenly, Jesus is flooded with another wave of memory, recalling His second trip to Skokie, 20 years earlier, in 1977. He hadn't anticipated returning so soon after His first visit in 1969. But a man leading a Midwestern chapter of a Nazi party offshoot was planning to march through town with his fellow white-supremacist followers. The purpose of the demonstration was not lost on Jesus, who was well-aware of the considerable number of Holocaust survivors populating the village. As if to make up for the lost summer of 1969, Jesus intervened, without even a single thought about gaining possible converts.

When the bus-driver turned into the Dempster Skokie Swift Depot, Jesus was amazed at how different it looked from the last time He had been there. He jotted a quick note about it along with a commendation to the architect for such a fine renovation and restoration.

A Chrysler, with the vanity plate SAVED, pulled alongside the bus at the intersection of Church Street and Skokie Boulevard. He could make out a Jesus fish decal in the back window, as well as a bumper sticker that read, "In Case of Rapture, This Vehicle Will Be Unattended." He shook His head, thinking to Himself, "Don't be so sure."

ACKNOWLEDGMENTS

The author gratefully acknowledges the editors and staff members of the various outlets in which work from *How to Whistle*, sometimes in different versions, previously appeared:

"6th & E" in *Men in Love* (Bold Strokes Books, 2016)

"Autographs" in *Blithe House Quarterly* (1997)

"Bathers" appeared as "Urban Desire '80" in *Thing* (1991)

"Bully in a Bar" in *Christopher Street* (1992) and *Bar Stories* (Alyson Books, 2000)

"Chocolate Dipped" in *Sex & Chocolate – Tasty Morsels For Mind and Body* (Paycock Press, 2006)

"Defending Karen Carpenter" in *Gargoyle 39/40* (1997)

"A Different Debra" in *Jonathan* (2015)

"Money Changing Hands" in *Blithe House Quarterly* (2001)

"My Mother's Vanity" in *Gargoyle 64* (2016)

"When Jesus Came Back to Skokie" in *Dissonance Magazine* (2020)

ABOUT THE AUTHOR

Gregg Shapiro is the author of seven books, including the expanded reissue of his short story collection *How to Whistle*. Since the 1980s his poetry and fiction have appeared in numerous literary journals, anthologies, and textbooks. A 1999 inductee into the Chicago LGBT Hall of Fame, Shapiro is an entertainment journalist, whose interviews and reviews run in a variety of regional LGBTQ+ and mainstream publications and websites. He lives in Fort Lauderdale, Florida with his husband Rick and their dog Coco.

Made in the USA
Middletown, DE
31 March 2021